College Life 101

KIM: The Party

COLLEGE LIFE 101

College Life 101

KIM: The Party

Wendy Corsi Staub

BERKLEY JAM BOOKS, NEW YORK

THE BERKLEY PUBLISHING GROUP
Published by the Penguin Group
Penguin Group (USA) Inc.
375 Hudson Street, New York, New York 10014, USA
Penguin Group (Canada), 10 Alcorn Avenue, Toronto, Ontario M4V 3B2, Canada
(a division of Pearson Penguin Canada Inc.)
Penguin Books Ltd., 80 Strand, London WC2R 0RL, England
Penguin Group Ireland, 25 St. Stephen's Green, Dublin 2, Ireland (a division of Penguin Books Ltd.)
Penguin Group (Australia), 250 Camberwell Road, Camberwell, Victoria 3124, Australia
(a division of Pearson Australia Group Pty. Ltd.)
Penguin Books India Pvt. Ltd., 11 Community Centre, Panchsheel Park, New Delhi—110 017, India
Penguin Group (NZ), Cnr. Airborne and Rosedale Roads, Albany, Auckland 1310, New Zealand
(a division of Pearson New Zealand Ltd.)
Penguin Books (South Africa) (Pty.) Ltd., 24 Sturdee Avenue, Rosebank, Johannesburg 2196,
South Africa

Penguin Books Ltd., Registered Offices: 80 Strand, London WC2R 0RL, England

This is a work of fiction. Names, characters, places, and incidents either are the product of the author's imagination or are used fictitiously, and any resemblance to actual persons, living or dead, business establishments, events, or locales is entirely coincidental.

COLLEGE LIFE 101
KIM: THE PARTY

A Berkley Jam Book / published by arrangement with the author

PRINTING HISTORY
Berkley edition / November 1997
Berkley Jam edition / April 2005

ISBN: 0-425-20188-0

BERKLEY® JAM BOOKS
Berkley Jam Books are published by The Berkley Publishing Group,
a division of Penguin Group (USA) Inc.,
375 Hudson Street, New York, New York 10014.
BERKLEY is a registered trademark of Penguin Group (USA) Inc.
BERKLEY JAM BOOKS and its logo are trademarks belonging to Penguin Group (USA) Inc.

PRINTED IN THE UNITED STATES OF AMERICA

10   9   8   7   6   5   4   3   2   1

For Kim,
with whom I've
attended many a wild party

And for Mark, Morgan, and Brody,
with love

Dear Allie (aka Birthday Girl-

Please excuse this card for being 1) late and 2) cheesy-it was the only one I could find in the drug-store that wasn't all flowery or didn't have one of those stupid "you're getting older" themes. I'm really sorry I missed your birthday-I thought of you on Columbus Day morning, but I went to this big costume party, and I got really wasted, and then it took me three days to recover! Anyway, I hope your birthday was fun and that you met some gorgeous guy and had wild sex. Just kidding! (at least, about the sex...unless you've drastically changed since I left town???) Give my regards to Weston Bay and all the neighbors-except Mrs. Anson, she still hates me!

Love ya,
Kim

Hey, Cameron:

See? I told you I'd send you this picture so you could see Jake, the guy I told you about on the phone the other night—the one who looks like Colin Farrell in <u>Alexander</u>. Anyway, it was taken at the Columbus Day costume party we had last week. As you can see, I went as Pocahontas, which some stupid guy told me was wrong because Columbus and Pocahontas weren't even alive at the same time. I was like, so what? It's just a party, not a history quiz. (Speaking of which, I'm about to fail my history class and Zara won't help me! Can you put in a good word with her for me?) Anyway, the guy dressed as Columbus with his arm around me in the picture is Jake. Pretty cute, huh? Don't you think he looks like Colin did when he was younger? He's really good friends with my housemate, Kevin, so he's around a lot. I'm going out with him next weekend, so I'll keep you posted.

Love,
me

P.S. Beryl and I and a few of our friends are planning a road trip to Florida in March, and we were wondering if we can crash with you. I wasn't sure if you'd still be living in the dorm, or if you'd be in your sorority house, but I figured you wouldn't mind some fun houseguests either way! I know it's five months away, but I wanted to make sure you don't make plans to do something boring like go home to Weston Bay. So let me know!

Zara:

I hope this is the right E-mail address! I know you couldn't find that history paper you wrote last year, but I was wondering if you'd mind checking again. I really need to borrow it, just to get some ideas for an essay. If you can find it, please send it to me as soon as you can! The essay was due last week! Thanks!

Kim

Dear Bridget

Here's that postcard I promised. What do you think of this aerial view of beautiful downtown Summervale, Indiana? I circled a house in the upper right-hand corner. It's on the corner of my street, about five doors down from my apartment building, which is cut out of the picture. Gee, I wonder why? Could it be too dumpy to be seen on a postcard? Not that I mind! I'm psyched just to be here! How are things in Seattle? Write and let me know how you're surviving without your beloved Grant! I told my mom to keep an eye on him for you, since she can see in his bedroom window from our front porch. She promised to report any suspicious activity! (Ha-ha)

Your bud,
Kim

Chapter 1

A shrill ringing sound woke Kim Garfield, shattering the silent room and painfully piercing her aching head.

"Oww," she groaned, burrowing into her pillow and feeling around for the crate that served as a makeshift bedside table. She found the clock radio and pounded the snooze button, but it immediately went off again.

What the ... ?

Oh, okay. It wasn't the alarm that was ringing.

She blinked, sat up, and looked around for the cordless phone. After pawing through the jumble of clothing and bedding surrounding her and coming up with nothing, she leaped out of bed, wincing as the motion jarred her throbbing skull.

Where the heck was the phone?

She glanced at the rumpled bed opposite hers. Her roommate, Beryl, was gone—poor thing had a mandatory-attendance class at, like, dawn on Fridays.

Following the sound of the ringing, Kim went from Beryl's bed to her dresser and hurriedly shoved aside a notebook, a sweatshirt, and several empty beer cans. No phone.

Where...?

There it was, peeking out from beneath Beryl's robe on the floor at the foot of Kim's bed. She grabbed it.

"Hello?" she said, pushing the Talk button and hoping to hear Jake's voice. He was supposed to call yesterday with details about their date tonight, and she still hadn't heard from him.

"Kim? Geez, I was about to hang up. What took you so long?"

"Allie?"

"Yeah." Her friend Allison DeMitri's voice sounded a little fuzzy, probably because the phone needed to be charged. No one ever bothered to put it back on the base—wherever that was kept. Kim made a mental note to look for it as soon as she hung up.

"Were you sleeping?" Allison asked.

"Yeah." She yawned and looked around for a clock. "What time is it?"

"Eleven-thirty. I just stopped home for lunch between classes. What are you doing in bed? Don't you have class?"

"No. I mean, yeah, I do, but it's just intro to anthropology. The professor doesn't take attendance."

"Shouldn't you be there anyway?"

"Nah. He doesn't even know who I am. It's in this huge lecture hall with about a thousand students."

"No, I mean shouldn't you go for your own benefit?" Allison clarified.

"Uh-uh. I'll just keep up with the reading and show up whenever he gives a test. There are only three per semester anyway, thank God."

"Oh." Her friend sounded slightly disapproving, which was to be expected.

Allison DeMitri was the kind of girl who did exactly what her parents and teachers expected of her.

Which explained why she was still living at home in Weston Bay, working her way through the local state university.

And why she was still, presumably, a virgin.

Kim yawned and stretched, and realized she was dressed in the jeans and sweater she'd worn to last night's fraternity party. Her hands and face felt grubby and she could smell cigarette smoke clinging to her hair. Yuck.

"I got your birthday card," Allison went on.

"Yeah? Sorry it was late."

"Actually, it wasn't. It was about a month early. My birthday's not until November."

"You're kidding." Kim frowned. "I thought it always fell on Columbus Day."

"No, it's usually around Veteran's Day."

"Are you sure?"

"Kim!" Allison laughed. "I swear I know when my birthday is. Believe me, it's next month."

"Oh. I just remembered we always had a long weekend off from school for your birthday."

"We did. But it wasn't in October. No big deal, though. I'll just save the card for next month."

"Good idea. No offense, but I probably won't remember to send another one." Kim rummaged through the clutter on her roommate's desk and found a lint-covered, half-empty pack of Life Savers. She popped one in her mouth, which tasted of the gin she'd downed last night.

"What are you eating?" Allison asked immediately. "Anything good?"

"Breakfast. A Pep-O-Mint Life Saver."

"Gee. Healthy, as usual."

"It's, like, the only thing in the house."

"Don't you guys buy groceries?"

"Not really. We're all broke."

"Even Beryl?"

"Her dad hasn't sent her a check lately. I think he's been on vacation with his new girlfriend or something."

"How about your other two roommates?"

"They're broke, too."

"Well, you can include me as a member of the Down and Out Club, too. I have about twenty cents to my name—as usual. What have you been up to since we talked last week?" Allison asked.

"Let's see ... last night, I went to a frat party—"

"Cute boys?"

"Mmm ... a few. The night before that, I went to a party. And the night before that—"

"Another party. I know." Allison sounded wistful. "Everyone's having a wild college experience except me."

"That's what you get for staying home," Kim said, and immediately regretted it. She knew, better than anyone, that Allison didn't have a choice.

Having grown up right next door to the DeMitri family, Kim was fully aware that Allison's parents didn't have a dime to spare on their oldest child's education.

Not that her own mother, Suzy, was much better off financially.

But as a teenager, Suzy Garfield had decided, upon giving birth to Kim, that her daughter would have the opportunity she herself would miss. She wanted Kim to go to college and make something of herself. And Suzy had worked two jobs most of her life to give Kim this chance for an education.

She'd even encouraged her daughter to go away to school, rather than staying home in Weston Bay, their small upstate New York hometown.

Kim—whose main criteria for college was that it be fun—had chosen the University of Indiana at Summervale based on two facts: her old hometown friend Beryl went there, and the school had a ratio of three men to every woman.

Besides that, it *was* an excellent school, with championship football and basketball teams and quite a few well-known alumni. The campus looked like something out of an old movie, the kind where wholesome young people frolicked against an idyllic backdrop of stately, ivy-covered buildings, shady trees, and fountains.

The only drawback was that the place was *huge*—both in acreage and in population. You could get lost pretty easily here, which, Kim was finding out, wasn't always such a bad thing.

"Believe me," Allison was saying, "I wouldn't be staying home and going to State if I could help it."

"I know you wouldn't. I'm sorry," Kim told her, crunching on the Life Saver.

"It's okay. If I'm lucky, I'll save enough money waitressing to move into the dorms next year. That would be a lot more bearable."

"Why don't you just get an apartment like me? It's cheaper. And you wouldn't have to deal with annoying dorm rules or a dining hall, and you could pick your roommate."

"I know, but I feel like I'd meet so many more people living in the dorms. And to me, that's the college experience. Having a roommate, eating in a dining hall...although I suppose I could turn out to have a hard time adjusting, the way Zara did."

"What do you mean?"

"Haven't you talked to her?"

"Nope. But I just sent her an E-mail, and she hasn't answered yet."

"Maybe you have the wrong address."

"Maybe. I probably should call her. I kind of need a favor," Kim said. "What's up with her, anyway?"

"Her roommate turned out to be this psycho pain in the

you-know-what, and she ended up moving out and getting a single."

"Really? I'd hate to live with a psycho, but living alone sounds boring," Kim observed.

"You know Zara. She likes the privacy so she can study. She also dropped out of pre-med."

"You're kidding!" Kim opened the top drawer of her dresser and looked for the bottle of Advil she'd thought she'd stashed there.

"Nope," Allison said. "Not kidding."

"Wow. Why'd she drop out?"

She could almost see Allison shrugging. "Who knows? Zara doesn't like to talk about her problems."

"Unlike me."

"What are your problems?"

"Where should I start?"

"That bad, huh?"

"Not really." Kim padded into the small, drab bathroom across the hall. The apartment was silent and Kevin and Monica's door was half open, which meant they were gone, too. "My biggest problem right now is that I have a major hangover, and I really need some ibuprofin."

"So find some."

"I'm looking." She opened the medicine cabinet and saw that it was just about empty, except for her housemate Monica's packet of birth control pills and a can of shaving cream and a razor that belonged to Monica's boyfriend, Kevin.

The room was damp and misty from someone's recent shower, and the toilet seat was up—thanks, no doubt, to Kevin. She noticed that the bathroom definitely needed cleaning. The toilet was gross, and the sink basin was covered with toothpaste stains and hair.

Kim made a face and propped the phone between her ear and shoulder as she washed her hands.

"What's that sound?" Allison asked.

"The water. I'm washing up. I feel totally grimy from last night. I guess I must have gone to bed without washing my hands or face or anything."

"You guess?"

"It's kind of blurry," Kim said. "The last thing I remember clearly is getting a suicide burrito with Beryl and eating it while we were walking home. I wonder what time *that* was. I feel like I've had only about two hours of sleep."

"I'll let you go back to bed then," Allison said. "I just wanted to thank you for the card."

"You're welcome—even though it was early. But you know me. I have a hard time keeping up with dates and holidays and stuff like that. Is there anyone else's birthday coming up that I should know about?"

"Grant's is on Halloween."

"Oh, right." That one was easy to remember. She had grown up going to Grant Caddaham's birthday parties, which were always elaborate affairs with costumes and apple bobbing and pumpkin decorating. Once, his parents had even hired a hay wagon to take everyone on rides up and down the street.

Grant had been one of those doted-upon only children.

Kim, who was also an only child, supposed she had also been doted upon—at least, as much as Suzy's limited income allowed.

"Do you want me to call you in two weeks to remind you to send him a card?" Allison asked.

"Somehow, Allie, sending Grant a card telling him to have a *happy* birthday just doesn't seem right this year. I mean, how happy can it be? His perfectly healthy forty-something-year-old father just dropped dead of a heart attack and his girl-friend is thousands of miles away."

"He is pretty miserable," Allison told her. "You know that old tire swing his dad hung in the tree in their side yard the summer we were eight?"

"The one you fell off that one time?" Kim asked. "You were screaming because you saw blood dripping down your leg. And me and Grant dialed 911, and about a zillion rescue ve-hicles pulled up in front. Remember?"

"I remember," Allison said ruefully. "I don't know why you guys just didn't go get someone instead."

"His mother was in the shower and couldn't hear us over the water, and mine wasn't home. And we were scared of yours. She was still mad at us for the hole we dug in your yard that time, looking for treasure. In fact, I swear she's still holding a grudge against me for that. And a lot of other things."

"Oh, Kim, don't be crazy."

But Allison's laugh, meant to be reassuring, sounded ner-vous, as if she'd hit the truth right on the head.

Kim knew Mrs. DeMitri couldn't stand her. She didn't approve of the fact that Suzy had never married Kim's father, didn't approve of Suzy's former career as a part-time topless dancer, and didn't approve of the men Suzy had dated—and married—over the years.

Kim would never forget the time, when she and Allison were in kindergarten, when Mrs. DeMitri had caught them playing dress-up with Suzy's lingerie. She'd been horrified to see Allison and Kim wearing black silk stockings, garter belts, and bustiers—not that they had the faintest clue of how to fasten any of it.

Mrs. DeMitri had banned Allison from the Garfield house and hadn't allowed her to play with Kim for a year. But somehow, slowly, things had drifted back to normal. You couldn't live next door to someone the same age—someone you liked and saw every day at school—and not be good friends. No matter what your parents wanted.

Kim had always sensed that Allison's mother was torn between feeling sorry for her—what with her wayward lifestyle and lack of a father—and wishing the Garfields would pick up and move out of the house next door to the DeMitris.

"So what about Grant and that tire swing?" she asked Allison. "I keep seeing him sitting out there in it, swinging."

"Maybe he just wants some fresh air," Kim suggested lamely.

"Yeah, right. He's alone, in the dark, Kim. He's really suffering, and I don't know if it's because he's grieving over his dad, or because he misses Bridget...."

"Both, most likely."

"I know. But he won't open up to me."

"He's never been the type to do that."

"Unlike me. I tell everyone everything. I should stop that now that I'm in college, huh? I mean, it's probably not a good idea to tell every guy I meet that I live at home here in town, and blah, blah, blah. Maybe that's why no one wants to go out with me. I'm scaring everyone away."

"You should really look into getting an apartment next semester, Allie."

"Next semester? No way. I'll be lucky if I can make tuition. And I'd better hang up so I can afford this phone call when the bill comes. My dad keeps warning me not to think I can call all over creation just because all my friends left town. Listen, Kim, you take care of yourself, okay? Be careful," Allison said, in the concerned, maternal tone she liked to use occasionally, even though she swore she never wanted to end up like her own mother. "Don't do anything too crazy out there in Indiana."

"I swear I won't go cow-tipping, Allie. At least, not every night. Maybe twice a week."

"Funny. You know what I mean."

"Don't worry. I'm just having fun."

"You always have fun. You're not always careful."

"Not true. So far, I haven't gotten arrested, pregnant, or killed."

"Geez, Kim. Don't even joke about that stuff."

"I wasn't joking. And Allie, lighten up. You need to make a road trip to Indiana and spend a few days learning how to relax, with me."

"Maybe I will."

"Let me know when, and I'll line up the cutest guys I can find."

Allison laughed and promised she'd work on it.

Kim hung up and set the phone on the back of the toilet seat, then stripped out of her clothes and jumped right into the shower. The pipes groaned and ran out of hot water within a minute.

She'd thought living in an old Victorian house would be kind of interesting, and it was. The small second-floor apartment had all sorts of old-fashioned quirks, like fireplaces in the bedrooms and built-in window seats and a laundry chute that led to the basement.

But there were drawbacks, too. Like no hot water or water pressure, ever.

And a bedroom window that was firmly stuck open a half an inch—it couldn't be lowered to shut out the draft and it couldn't be raised to let in a breeze.

And, Kim suspected, there were mice. Not that she'd ever seen one. But she'd heard gnawing sounds in the walls, and she'd found some suspicious brown pellet-type droppings on her closet floor.

Now, as she stepped out of the shower, she thought optimistically that things could be worse. Much worse.

Her housemates were terrific.

Well, Beryl was.

She'd known Beryl Starmeyer forever. Beryl had been a year ahead of Kim all through the Weston Bay public school system—one of those early-to-mature girls who had started smoking in sixth grade and having sex in seventh. She was nearly six feet tall and had a model's looks—had even done some modeling back in high school, when her figure was stick-thin.

Kim had always looked up to Beryl, who offered her what her other friends—Allison and Bridget and Cameron and Zara—couldn't:

Wisdom.

And the wild side.

It was Beryl who had taught Kim how to sneak vodka from her mother's liquor cabinet and replace it with water.

And Beryl who had advised Kim, last year, to switch from the diaphragm her mother's gynecologist had supplied to birth control pills. "They're way more reliable," she'd said knowingly.

And thanks to Beryl, she was here at Summervale. All through Kim's senior year at Weston Bay, she'd been tantalized by tales of Beryl's fun-filled life away at college. She'd learned that U. of I. at Summervale had a reputation for being a "party school," where the social scene took precedence over academics.

And that was right up Kim's alley.

She'd maintained a B average in high school—not because she'd studied. Ever.

No, Kim had been blessed with natural intelligence that meant she had a borderline genius IQ. She was also a classic underachiever, according to her teachers and the guidance counselor, who had pressured her to excel.

She had no desire to excel.

All Kim wanted, all she'd *ever* wanted, was to have fun and be happy.

And so far, all her life—and particularly in the past month since she'd arrived at Summervale—she'd succeeded.

She and Beryl had been having a blast.

And she couldn't even complain about Kevin and Monica, because it wasn't that she didn't like them. They were just... different.

Monica was okay, she supposed, when Kevin wasn't around. She was a tiny waif with pale skin, morose-looking gray eyes, and long, lifeless, drab blond hair. When Kim had first met her she'd thought maybe she was sick, but it turned out she always looked that way.

Kevin had the same general pallor, although he wore his blond hair pulled back in a ponytail and his eyes were usually bright—*too* bright. Kim suspected he was stoned most of the time. He rarely spoke, and when he did, it was usually to utter some sardonic, pseudo-intellectual observation.

Apparently Monica thought he was hilarious and a genius, because she hung on his every word, quoted him to everyone who would listen, and generally kissed his butt all day, every day.

Kim had no idea what Monica saw in him, but she knew what Kevin saw in her. Who wouldn't want a girlfriend who took care of his every need and whim? Monica did Kevin's laundry, cleaned up after him—when she bothered to clean up at all—and even did most of his schoolwork.

It made Kim nauseated to watch her, but as Beryl pointed out, Kevin and Monica's relationship was their business. They were easy roommates, since they were hardly ever around, and when they were, they were usually holed up behind their closed bedroom door.

Kim grabbed someone's damp towel from the hook on the wall beside the tub and wrapped it around herself. She never remembered to bring one in with her, and there was no place to store anything in the cramped bathroom.

Scooping up her clothes from where she'd dropped them beside the toilet, Kim accidentally knocked the telephone from the back of the bowl.

It landed in the toilet with a splash.

"Eeeuuuhh," Kim said, surveying it for a moment.

She debated leaving it there for one of her roommates to find and fish out. They'd all been pretty messed up last night—no one would realize she was the one who'd dropped it in.

But then she remembered Jake.

How was he going to call her if the phone was submerged in the depths of the toilet?

She started singing her favorite Eminem song at the top of her lungs—for some reason, it helped—and plunged her hand into the icy water to retrieve the receiver.

Wrapping it in another damp towel she found on the doorknob, she dried it off, then pushed Talk to see if she'd still get a dial tone.

Miraculously there was one.

Carrying the phone, she made her way back to the bedroom, noting that the hallway floor outside her room was sticky beneath her bare feet.

She vaguely remembered Beryl spilling a drink there a few nights ago. Something green... oh, right. It had been one of those bottled Margaritas that didn't taste like the real thing, but were better than beer in a pinch.

In her room Kim lit a Salem and smoked it while she got dressed in jeans and sneakers. She borrowed Beryl's thick gray sweatshirt emblazoned with the Summervale crest, which was a mile too long for her, since it was even oversized on Beryl. But most of Kim's clothes were dirty, in a pile on the floor.

Doing laundry hadn't seemed like a priority until now. She vowed to head to the Laundromat down the street as soon as she got a chance.

She combed some gel through her shoulder-length, thick blond hair, then left it to dry naturally. Somehow, it always came out halfway decent when she did that. Her friends back home had always pointed out she had great hair, which she totally appreciated.

She also had a naturally thin figure, for which she was also grateful. Good metabolism came in handy, especially lately, when everyone around her kept complaining about putting on weight. Beryl had gained twelve pounds since last year and kept going on starvation diets.

Kim had never been on a diet in her life, and if she was anything like her mother, she'd never have a weight problem.

She debated putting on makeup, and decided not to bother until later. She knew she was lucky her skin wasn't totally messed up, the way she kept going to bed with makeup on. Luckily, her complexion had always been decent. But it wouldn't stay that way if she didn't start washing her face at night, not to mention eating a healthier diet.

It was just so hard, though. Both the washing and the eating.

She was always exhausted when she got home in the wee hours from wherever she'd been—and there was always someplace interesting to be. She hadn't spent one night at home since she'd arrived at school.

And there certainly just wasn't time to go out and buy fruits and vegetables, or whatever it was she should be eating. Her diet lately consisted of pizza and tortilla chips and burgers...and liquor.

She probably shouldn't be drinking so much, she thought, examining her face in the mirror. She half-expected her green eyes to be bloodshot, but they were as clear as ever. And her face wasn't pale, or sunken, or anything.

No, she was fortunate enough not to show, on the outside, what she felt like on the inside.

You'd never know, seeing her perky, pretty face, that she felt like some gnome was living behind the bridge of her nose, chipping away at her cranium with a sledgehammer. Her stomach was hollow and queasy. And her legs felt wobbly, as though she needed to either eat or sleep.

Probably both.

With a sigh, she opted for food.

Unfortunately, the kitchen cupboards were bare, except for a few slices of moldy bread, four packages of chicken-flavored curly oriental noodles, and the chili powder and minced onion flakes Monica had bought for some Mexican recipe she kept promising to make some night.

Kim hated cooking, but she decided she was hungry enough to make a package of noodles. According to the directions on the back of the wrapper, all you had to do was boil a certain amount of water, dump everything in, and wait, like, two minutes.

"I can do that," she said aloud, running the water, then returning to the cupboard for a measuring cup. All she could find was a chipped coffee mug.

She refilled it twice, dumping the water into a battered kettle, and spent five minutes trying to get the stove burner to light.

Finally she figured it out and a few minutes later was pouring a steaming serving of noodles into a warped plastic bowl.

They were a little mushy, she discovered. And the broth had absolutely zero flavor. She wondered if maybe the coffee mug she'd used to measure had been bigger than a regular cup.

The apartment door slammed as she was hunting through a drawer for some salt or pepper packets she'd thought she'd seen there.

A masculine voice called, "Hey, Kevin? You around, man?"

"He's not here," Kim said, getting up to go see who it was.

A guy stood there in the hallway, holding the front wheel of a bicycle.

He was thin—skinny, really—and had long brown hair that straggled past his shoulders. His nose was on the big side but his eyes were really nice—a piercing, startling blue. He wore jeans, holey black sneakers, and a purple tie-dyed hooded shirt.

He'd be kind of cute if he wasn't so scrawny, Kim decided.

"You Kevin's housemate?" the guy asked.

"Yup. I'm Kim."

"I'm Random."

"You're who?"

"Random," he said, spelling it for her.

That was what she'd thought he'd said. Huh.

"You know, it's my nickname," he clarified. "Get it?"

"Got it."

"Where is he?"

"Kevin?" She shrugged. "Class, or maybe work."

"Can't be work. He got fired the other night."

"Oh, yeah."

She had almost forgotten about that. She remembered that she and Beryl had come home, drunk, to find Kevin bumming because he'd been caught stealing food from the restaurant where he worked as a dishwasher.

"It was just a steak," he'd said, shaking his head wistfully. "It wasn't even a good cut. Just a stinkin' hunk of chuck."

For some reason, she and Beryl had found that hilariously funny. They kept screaming, "Just a stinkin' hunk of chuck!" and then collapsing in laughter.

Kevin hadn't appreciated their reaction. He kept shaking his head dejectedly and mumbling that he didn't know how he was going to pay his rent and tuition now.

"Listen," his tie-dyed friend said to Kim, "can you give Kev something for me?"

"Sure. You mean the wheel?"

"Huh? Oh, this?" He held up the bike tire. "Nah, this is mine."

"Yeah? Why are you carrying it around?"

"In this neighborhood, you can't leave your bike outside for a second. Someone'll take it."

"Lock it."

"Doesn't matter. They'll get it anyway."

"Are you serious? Even with a lock?"

"Crummy neighborhood," the guy said with a shrug. "You never know."

"I don't think it's that crummy," Kim said. "I mean, it's run-down, but it's not, like, ridden with crack houses or anything."

The guy raised an eyebrow at her. "You'd be surprised. You shouldn't leave your door unlocked."

"I didn't."

"It was unlocked, man."

"Well, someone must have left without locking it." Actually, she'd never stopped to worry about whether the door was locked or not. She had keys, but rarely took them with her, and as far as she knew, neither did her housemates.

She'd always felt totally safe here.

Now it occurred to her that some psycho rapist serial killer could just stroll in off the streets.

Like this guy, Random, had.

She eyed him warily.

"Listen," he said, a little impatiently, "here's the package for Kevin. Make sure you give it to him personally, okay?" He flung a small, crumpled paper bag at her.

She caught it. "What is it?"

He studied her briefly, as if debating whether to tell her.

And in that moment she knew what was in the package.

"Just some, uh, cupcakes my girlfriend baked for him," the guy said with a wink. "Don't smush them now, okay?"

"Yeah, right. Cupcakes. I won't smush them," Kim said, shaking her head. She watched as the guy left and went to lock the door behind him, only to discover the bolt didn't slide all the way over.

She'd have to alert the landlord, whoever he was. Beryl must know, since she was the one who'd found the place. Kim made a mental note to ask her about it.

She went down the hall to Kevin and Monica's room, opened the door, and tossed the package onto their rumpled bed.

She knew they got high a lot. In fact, Beryl did, too, but not as much. The three of them had gotten stoned when Kim was around a few times, before they went out, and they'd seemed surprised when she had refused the joint they'd passed around.

It wasn't that Kim was a prude about pot or anything. She didn't care if other people used it. She just didn't like it. Not the smell, or the way it had made her feel the few times she'd tried it, or the fact that it was illegal.

Actually, when it came right down to it, so was booze, if you were underage. And she was.

But Kim could handle liquor. It was fun, and it wasn't dangerous. She never lost control of herself with liquor...

And she liked to be in control.

Well, okay, there were a few times, back in junior high when she'd first started drinking, that she'd gotten weepy, crying, sloppy drunk.

But these days that didn't happen.

And she drew the line at drugs, though if other people, people she knew, wanted to use them, that was fine with her.

So what Kevin did with whatever was in the package on his bed was none of her business.

Still, for some reason, she felt a little uneasy for the first time in ages.

About her living situation, and about being on her own, and so far away from home.

Which was totally unexpected, because Kim liked to think that she took things in stride. She always had.

She'd been through two marriages and two divorces with her mother, and none of that supposedly traumatic domestic upheaval had fazed her.

Of course, they'd always lived in the same small bungalow on working-class Finch Street in Weston Bay, surrounded by the same stuff and the same friends.

It was the stepfathers who came and went.

First there had been Alan Carmichael, whom Suzy had met at a Grateful Dead concert and married on impulse the next day. That had lasted only a year, and Suzy had thrown a big party when the divorce was finalized.

Next came John Beetes, a widower with three teenaged kids. All four of them had moved into the house on Finch Street, filling every inch of space with clutter and pets and noise. Kim, three years younger than John's youngest daughter, had felt pushed aside and trampled over, and it had been a relief when Suzy told her she and John were splitting up. He didn't want a wife; he wanted a housekeeper and nanny for his kids. Which was a joke, because Suzy was hardly the homey type.

Before and after Alan and John, there had been a parade of boyfriends, some live-in; most not. Kim had never questioned her mother's lifestyle; had never minded it.

Basically, she'd learned that, in life, some people—mostly men—came and went. Others—mostly women—were there for the duration.

Like her mother.

And her friends.

She felt a pang, suddenly, missing Cameron and Allison and Bridget and Zara.

And her mother.

Yes, especially Suzy.

She thought of calling home, but realized her mother would be at work, typing some boring letter or filing some boring folder at the insurance office where she worked during the day.

And after that she would be off to the Upwind Café on

the outskirts of Weston Bay, where she was a cocktail waitress five nights a week.

All of that—two demanding, exhausting jobs—just to make sure Kim had a chance to go to school and make something of herself.

Kim swallowed hard over the lump in her throat, wishing she could tell her mother how much she appreciated what she had done...

And how much she missed her.

But Suzy was at work, and her boss didn't like her to receive personal calls, so there was nothing Kim could do.

And anyway, she and Suzy didn't usually go in for that sappy, heart-to-heart mother-daughter stuff.

Forcing herself to shrug as if she didn't have a care in the world, she went into the small living room and turned on the stereo, blasting a U2 CD that was guaranteed to banish the slightest trouble.

Then she returned to the kitchen, where her cold, flavorless, soggy noodles were waiting.

Chapter 2

"Jake," Kim said, licking her cookies 'n' cream ice cream cone, "is a jerk."

"I totally agree." Beryl tossed her short, glossy black hair and slurped her Skinny-Minny, a disgusting—in Kim's opinion—concoction made from two scoops of some synthetic nonfat ice-cream substitute and a squirt of chalky-looking fake chocolate syrup.

"How is that stuff?" Kim asked as Beryl swirled her straw in the plastic cup and made a face.

"Hideous. How would you think it would be? Do you know how lucky you are to be able to eat whatever you want?"

"Yup." Kim caught a drip with her tongue, then pulled a napkin out of the dispenser on the table.

They were in the Hop, a local diner masquerading as some trendy retro-fifties-style hangout, complete with a jukebox filled with forty-year-old bebop music. The decor was overkill, in Kim's opinion—pink vinyl booths, black-and-white tile floors, and everywhere, posters of Marilyn and Elvis.

But the food was decent, and cheap—a definite plus.

"I can't believe he didn't call you," Beryl commented.

"Who, Jake? I know. The other night he was all over me. I thought he really liked me, and he made such a *thing* about how he wanted to take me to dinner at some great restaurant. I mean, why ask someone out and get her hopes up if you have no intention of following through?"

"Because he wanted to sleep with you." Beryl's observation was made in her bland, Beryl-way, in a matter-of-fact tone and punctuated with a shrug.

"You mean, he wanted to sleep with me that night, after the party?"

"Yeah. I think he was really into your Pocahontas outfit. It was incredibly skimpy."

"Well, that was for historic authenticity, not to show off my cleavage—what little there is."

"Yeah, right."

"Beryl! I'm not a slut."

"Did anyone say you were? And anyway, I think Jake figured that out when you wouldn't go home with him. And he asked you out for this weekend *before* that, remember?"

"You think if I had slept with him that night, he would have followed through with the date?"

"Nope." Beryl sipped more Skinny-Minny. "I think he's an asshole who wanted to get laid. Period."

"Well, the next time I see him, I'm going to tell him what I think of him."

"As if he'll care."

"So? It'll make me feel better," Kim decided. "I mean, what did he think, that I'd spend Friday night sitting home waiting for the phone to ring?"

"You did."

"So? He doesn't know that. And *you're* not going to tell him."

Beryl shook her head.

"I can't believe I missed Gregg and Phil's cookout for him. I was really looking forward to that."

"Believe me, it wasn't that great," Beryl said. "Mostly girls were there. And I woke up feeling totally nauseated this morning. I still don't feel good. I don't think Gregg cooked the burgers all the way."

"Really?" Kim raised a brow at her. "I hope you don't have that E. coli thing."

"What thing?"

"That bacteria that kills people," Kim said. "You know, in raw hamburgers."

Beryl shoved her cup aside and clutched her stomach. "It kills people?"

"God, where have you been? Haven't you heard about it?"

"No..."

"One burger, and you could just..." Kim drew her forefinger across her throat.

"Oh, my God. I can't believe I didn't even realize I was eating something that could be deadly."

"Yeah, and even if Phil's burgers weren't, that Skinny-Minny brew probably is." Kim was teasing her now, but Beryl wasn't smiling.

"I think I have to go to the bathroom." Beryl slid out of the booth and made her way toward the door marked DAMES at the back of the restaurant.

Kim licked her ice cream, bored, and glanced around. She spotted a semi-decent-looking guy with a familiar face up near the register and tried to think of how she knew him.

She couldn't remember. Maybe she was wrong.

His eyes collided with hers, and he grinned and waved.

So she wasn't wrong. He knew her, too.

Who was he?

He was kind of lanky and somewhat nondescript. No interesting items of clothing or a even haircut that made a statement. He wore plain Levi's 501s and a short-sleeved white Gap Pocket Tee. His hair was just brown and short and... well, combed.

"Hi," he called, after accepting his change and a white paper bag from the cashier.

Is he talking to me?

"How's it going?" he asked.

Apparently, he was.

"Oh... uh, it's going great."

Please don't let him come over here. I have no idea who he is, and I'm not in the mood—

"Hey, your hair looks good like that. Don't you usually wear it down?"

Kim grinned.

Please let him come over here. He seems really nice and he is pretty cute in a straitlaced sort of way....

"I French-braided it," she told him, reaching up to pat her hair. "It was so sticky out today, I didn't want it all over my neck."

"It is pretty hot for October."

Oh, good. Here he comes.

"Not so much hot," Kim told him as he sauntered over, "but it's humid, you know?"

"Yeah. It is humid."

Awkward moment of silence.

Kim scrambled for something to say. "Well, it's probably snowing already back where I'm from."

"Where's that? Buffalo?"

Her jaw dropped. "Close enough. I'm from Weston Bay, New York—it's about a half hour from Buffalo. How'd you guess?"

"The accent. My brother-in-law is from there, and you sound just like him."

"Hey, I don't have an accent."

"See? The way you said *have* and the way you said *accent* with the flat *a*—that's an accent."

"What do you mean?" She wasn't sure if she was amused or annoyed.

"You say it like it's two syllables. Hay-ave."

"I do not!"

"Okay, you don't." He gave an easygoing grin. "I'm from New York, too—downstate—and half the time my room-mate, who's from Chicago, can't figure out what I'm saying."

"Where in New York?"

"Westchester County. Scarsdale?" he added, like he was wondering if she'd heard of it.

Who hadn't heard of Scarsdale?

Who didn't know that people who lived there were very well-off? Maybe not every last one of them, but for the most part, Kim figured, people from Scarsdale were wealthy.

And something about this guy spoke of money, despite his simple clothes.

"Do you know where that is?"

"Scarsdale? Not really." She licked her ice cream.

More silence. Not so awkward, though, somehow.

He filled it. "So your name's Kim, right?"

"Right."

And I have no clue who you are.

"I'm Joe. I've seen you in my history class."

"Oh, right," she said, even though she didn't remember seeing him there. She'd only gone twice—on the first day, and for a quiz two weeks ago.

"Have you been sick lately?"

"Me? No. Why—"

"You haven't been in class."

"Oh. I know." She took a nibbling bite out of her cone,

careful not to let the ice cream spill through the gap. "I just . . . I mean, attendance isn't required, and I figured if I just keep up with the reading, I'll be fine."

"I guess. But why not go to lecture? You're missing out. Dr. Armstrong's really an interesting professor. Her great-great-great-grandfather was a Civil War general."

"Really?"

"Weren't you there the day she told us that? I think it was the first day."

Kim probably had been there, but she must not have been paying attention. She said, "I'm sure Dr. Armstrong's very interesting, but I've been really busy with other stuff. . . ."

"Like . . . ?"

"You know . . ."

Sleeping. Drinking. Watching reruns of The Real World *and* Road Rules *on MTV.*

He seemed to be waiting for her reply.

Kim caught an ice-cream drip with her tongue and decided this Joe guy was irritating, the way he acted like she should be telling him all these intimate details of her life.

"If you want to come on Monday, I'll save you a seat," he offered.

"Oh . . . well, maybe I will."

He *did* have a nice grin, kind of wide and extra-happy, revealing straight white teeth. He must have worn braces as a kid, she decided. No one naturally had teeth like that.

"What topic did you choose for your paper?"

"What paper?"

He looked at her as though she were out of it. "The one on the Civil War? I did mine on the Underground Railroad."

"Oh. Mine's going to be on Reconstruction."

If I ever get it from Zara.

"You didn't turn yours in yet?"

"No . . . I got an extension."

Which was a lie. But maybe she should go see the professor and see if she could get one. She could say she'd been sick or something. . . .

"Who're you here with?" Joe had spied Beryl's Skinny-Minny on the table.

"My housemate. She's in the ladies' room."

Was it Kim's imagination, or did he seem relieved? Had he been thinking she might be on a date with some guy? Was he glad she wasn't?

Are you out of your mind?

Joe Whoever wasn't her type. Too straight-arrow.

Even if he was nice to talk to.

"There she is now," Kim observed as the Dames door opened and Beryl, looking pale and disheveled, walked out.

"She doesn't look so good," Joe commented.

"She doesn't feel so good." She took another bite of her cone.

"Maybe she has that stomach flu thing that's going around the dorms."

"We don't live in the dorms."

"Really? Where do you live?"

"In an apartment. On West Twelfth Street."

"Isn't that over by the meat-packing factory?"

"Yeah." She saw the look on his face. "The neighborhood's not *that* bad. Is it, Beryl?"

Her roommate blinked. "Huh?"

"Never mind. This is Joe. Joe, Beryl."

"Nice to meet you," he said politely.

"You, too." She looked distracted and sat down across from Kim.

"Well . . ." Joe shifted his weight. "Better get back to work."

"You're working?" That was surprising. She'd had him pegged as a lazy rich kid. "Where?"

"The music store next door. Tambourine Man. It's really fun. Two of my buddies work there, too. Great perks. We get to listen to new CDs and we get excellent concert tickets."

So he just did it for kicks, she thought—not because he really needed the money.

"I'm on lunch break," he added, holding up the white paper bag.

"What are you having?" Kim asked.

"A burger. Fries."

"A burger?" Beryl shuddered. "Watch out for that A-colic stuff."

"Huh?" Joe looked confused.

"She means E. coli. The bacteria," Kim told him.

"Oh." He grinned. "Thanks for the warning. See you guys."

"See you." Kim watched him walk away, thinking that his butt looked pretty good in faded Levi's. That was one of her personal tests for guys. That, and whether they had strong jawlines. She liked a guy with a chiseled jaw.

She hadn't noticed whether Joe had one.

Not that it mattered.

He wasn't her type.

She turned her attention back to Beryl. "How are you feeling?"

"Lousy. I barfed. Do you have a mint?"

"No. How could you barf?"

"I started thinking about raw hamburger squirming with some disgusting creepy-crawling bacteria, and it was easy."

Kim rolled her eyes and popped the last of her cone into her mouth. "You ready to go?"

"Definitely. Let's stop and get a six-pack on the way home."

"I thought you were sick."

"I barfed. I'm not sick. And I'll feel better if I have a beer. Carbonated beverages are supposed to settle a person's stomach."

"That's seltzer, not beer."

"Well, anyway, it's Saturday."

Kim shrugged, deciding she wouldn't mind having a beer herself.

"Do you ever feel like all we ever do is drink?" she asked Beryl as they walked out onto the street. She lit a cigarette.

"So? What's wrong with drinking? We're in college, Kim. That's what we're supposed to do."

"You're right." She offered the pack of Salems to Beryl,

who took one even though she had asthma and rarely smoked.

As they passed the music shop next door to the Hop, Kim found herself peeking in the window for a glimpse of Joe . . .

And disappointed when she didn't see him.

Which was odd.

Because he definitely wasn't her type.

Definitely not.

"What about the one in the black shirt? Beryl asked Kim over the blasting White Stripes song.

Kim squinted across the frat house living room. "The one by the keg or the one holding the chubby redhead's hand?"

"The one by the keg! The other one's obviously taken."

"Yeah, but he's cuter. The one by the keg isn't my type."

"He has long hair. You said you like long hair."

"Yeah, but his is all skeevy. You know, straggly. Like he just got up."

"So? Maybe he did." Beryl rolled her eyes and sipped her beer from the sixteen-ounce plastic cup she was holding. "You're too picky, Kim. You're telling me that no one at this party is your type?"

She looked around. "I kind of like the guy over there by the door. . . ."

"The one who looks like Jude Law?"

"Yeah. Except I hate his shoes."

"Really? I love his shoes. I hate *my* shoes," Beryl said, looking down at her feet. "Why did I wear these chunky heels? I feel like I'm towering above everyone."

"You're not *that* tall," Kim comforted her.

"I am so. And in these shoes, I dwarf everyone in the room."

"Not that guy." Kim pointed at a bearded giant who had to be at least six-foot-five. She and Beryl laughed.

"We have to find boys tonight," Beryl said, slurring slightly. "Cute boys."

"Cute boys," Kim agreed. "Tonight."

They clicked their plastic beer glasses together.

"Here's to us," Beryl said.

"And those like us," Kim said.

"Damn few left," they concluded in unison, and laughed.

It was their usual toast.

"You guys, have you seen Kevin?" Monica appeared, looking harried.

The three of them had come over together from the apartment, and Monica had left a note for Kevin to meet her here, at the party.

Kim and Beryl told her they hadn't seen him.

"I can't deal with this," Monica said. "He's getting totally unreliable. He was supposed to be home at nine to go out with us."

"Where was he?" Kim asked.

"Over at Jake's, getting stoned."

"Jake's?" Kim echoed. "What's up with him, anyway? He was supposed to call me to go out on a date this weekend."

Earlier, she'd avoided mentioning him to Monica, not wanting her friend to tell Kevin—and Kevin to tell Jake—that she was upset over being stood up.

Now, after who-knew-how-many beers, she wasn't as concerned about discretion when it came to Jake the Jerk.

"A date?" Monica smirked. "I told you the other day, Kim. Jake doesn't *date*, no matter what he said to you that night. All I've ever seen him do is get messed up and try to scam an easy lay."

"Nice," Beryl commented, sipping her beer.

"Is he coming to this party with Kevin?"

Monica shrugged. "Probably. If he's still, like, conscious."

"If he does," Kim said, "I'm going to tell him that it was really horrible of him to do that to me."

"You are not," Beryl informed her.

"I'm not?"

"No. You'll look like a pathetic, desperate, whiny loser. You have to act like you don't care."

"I don't care."

"Yeah, right," Monica said, shoving her lank hair back from her face and keeping an eye on the door.

"I don't. Not about Jake. Even though he *is* my type—I mean, he would be if he weren't such a jerk. I just care that some nobody guy would think he could just ask me out on a date, going on and on about where he's going to take me and how we're going to get all dressed up and everything, and then just drop the whole thing."

"Welcome to the real world," Beryl said. "*All* guys are jerks."

"Not Joe," Kim told her.

"Joe?" Beryl repeated. "Joe who?"

"Who's Joe?" Monica asked.

Kim blinked. "He's this guy in one of my classes. Beryl met him."

"I did?"

"Today, at the Hop."

"I didn't meet any—oh, the burger guy?"

"Burger guy?" Monica looked confused.

"Yeah, him," Kim said, nodding. "*He's* not a jerk."

"How do you know?" Beryl asked.

"He just doesn't seem like one. He's the opposite of Jake. He's, like, a fine upstanding citizen. Unlike Jake, who's a lousy, standing-up citizen." She cracked up. "Get it? Upstanding? Standing-up? As in, Jake stood me up?"

Beryl and Monica didn't seem to find that nearly as hilarious as Kim did.

"So if the burger guy's so terrific, you should go out with him," Monica advised. "Can I bum a cigarette?"

Kim stopped laughing and offered her pack to Monica, then lit one herself before saying, "Joe's not my type. Too boring. But definitely not a jerk."

"Only exciting jerks are her type," Beryl told Monica.

"Yeah, join the club. I didn't think Kevin was a jerk, but—hey, look! There he is."

"Joe?" Kim swiveled her head, looking toward the door in the direction where Monica was pointing.

"No, *duh.* Kevin." Her friend started in his direction.

"Yeah, and look who's with him," Beryl said to Kim.

"Jake. He looks pretty hot, huh?" Kim took in Jake's broad shoulders beneath his black-and-gray plaid flannel shirt, his devil-may-care grin, the cocky way he tossed his long sandy-colored hair.

"You're right," Beryl said, peering at him. "He really does look like Colin Farrell did in _Alexander_. Kind of dangerous and rugged..."

"God, I think I have to have him."

"Kim! You do not."

Kim sipped her beer and vaguely thought she should really stop drinking. She should get a Coke or something. Did they even _have_ Coke around? She hadn't seen anything but beer....

And beer was going down so easily.

"Think of what he did to you," Beryl was saying.

"Yeah, you're right."

"Think of how you spent all last night at home alone, waiting for him to call."

"Yeah, I know."

They both took another sip.

"You want him anyway, don't you," Beryl said, watching her with a resigned look.

"Definitely. Come on, let's go see Monica and Kevin." Kim grabbed Beryl's arm and dragged her across the room, crashing into people as they went. She was too tipsy to care.

In the back of her mind she thought that maybe this wasn't such a good idea....

Approaching Jake when she was so wasted.

What if she said something she'd regret?

What if she *did* something she'd regret?

Too late now.

Jake had turned in her direction, his slightly glassy eyes lighting up as he caught sight of her.

I'll just be really, really careful.

And this will be my last beer, I swear.

"*Oh*, my God, Beryl, my head is—"

Kim cut herself off in midsentence, opening her eyes and seeing that Beryl wasn't in the room.

Actually, *the room* wasn't in the room—at least, not the one she had been expecting to see.

Her room, the one she shared with Beryl.

No, she wasn't home. She was in a strange place, lying in a strange bed, with . . .

Okay, not with a stranger, thank God, she saw as she turned her head and recognized the sleeping face beside her.

This was Jake.

Beautiful Jake, whose face was covered with a thin growth of stubble and whose gorgeous blue eyes were closed as he slept peacefully, snoring slightly through his nose.

Kim thought back to last night . . .

The party . . .

Dancing with Jake in a dark corner of the frat house, even after the music stopped playing.

Slow dancing...

Making out...

Leaving.

Walking...

Or had they driven?

Kim squeezed her eyes shut, trying to remember.

Major memory blanks.

Now here she was, with Jake, in what was apparently Jake's room...

In Jake's bed...

Naked?

No, she realized, feeling under the nubby, musty-smelling Indian wool blanket that was covering them.

Okay, good. She was still wearing her shirt and jeans from last night.

And Jake...

She felt his chest.

He didn't even flinch or miss a beat with his snoring.

Jake wasn't wearing a shirt, but...

Yes, good. He had his jeans on.

So she hadn't slept with him.

Or had she?

If I did, would I have gotten dressed again afterward, and then gone to sleep here?

Would he have gotten dressed again?

Highly doubtful.

Kim lifted her head, then almost put it back down on the pillow again when a searing pain shot through her skull.

Advil.

She needed Advil.

And water.

And food.

Something starchy and heavy, like a big platter of hash browns.

Jake stirred and rolled over, away from her, taking the covers with him.

Kim sat up, feeling dizzy, and pushed herself off his bed, looking around the room as she stood.

It was pretty bare, except for his beat-up wooden bed and a matching dresser. On the dresser was a lamp and a stack of textbooks, two prescription bottles of pills, and a bong.

The walls were painted a dingy purple-black color. There were a few posters of naked women scattered about.

The floor was covered in nondescript carpeting that was either light gray or blue, and littered with beer cans and crumpled wrappers and clothes.

And the room smelled musty and stale and gross, like dirty laundry.

Beautiful Jake, it seemed, lived like a slob.

Not that Kim was a perfect little happy homemaker, but still...

It kind of shattered the myth.

And so did his snoring, which she could hear from beneath the blanket he'd pulled over his head.

She ran her fingers through her hair and picked her way to the door, finding herself in a long hallway lined with doors.

She knew he lived in a house on West Fifth Street with a couple of other guys, and she wasn't particularly anxious to run into any of them right now.

She moved along the corridor, turned a corner, went down a flight of stairs, and found herself in a cluttered living room. Someone was snoring on the couch, huddled beneath a crocheted afghan. The television was on; a perky MTV VJ chattering about something.

Kim scurried past to the door, letting herself out.

The morning was gray and drizzly.

The street was deserted.

She stopped at the corner to get her bearings, then headed toward home, remembering what Kevin's friend Random had said about the neighborhood.

Well, I doubt anyone would consider mugging or raping me now, Kim decided. She was totally disheveled, without even a jacket or purse. Her head was pounding and her mouth tasted awful.

How much had she drunk last night?

A lot.

That much was obvious.

But it had been fun. . . .

At least, what she remembered of it.

She just wished she remembered more.

Like what had happened with Jake.

Should she have woken him?

Said good morning?

Said goodbye?

That would depend, she decided, on what had happened between them.

She hoped nothing happened she hadn't wanted to have happen.

This isn't good, she decided, crossing a street hurriedly to get out of the way of an oncoming car.

It passed, and she saw a family of churchgoers—Mother, Father, Sis, and Brother, too, all of them apparently dressed in Sunday best—staring out the car windows at her in...what? Dismay? Disgust?

They probably think I'm some hooker, Kim realized, *stumbling home after a busy night.*

No, of course they didn't think that.

After all, she wasn't dressed like a hooker.

Was she?

How did hookers dress?

Oh, God, did she look like a hooker?

And while she was on the subject...had she become a slut?

She had no idea.

How was she supposed to find out?

Call Jake and say, "Excuse me, I was wondering if we slept together last night?"

How pathetic.

What would her friends back home think? She knew they thought she was wild—

Hell, compared to them, she *was* wild.

But she wasn't a slut.

She had slept with exactly three people in her life.

Two had been serious boyfriends; the third, a summer fling she'd had with an older guy, a musician. She'd met him last summer while she was working as a counselor at Camp Timberlake.

She'd slept with him on the first date, too.

But that wasn't like *this*.

Not like getting totally wasted and hooking up with some guy at a party...

A jerky guy who'd already burned you.

Kim walked faster, then realized she was practically running along the sidewalk. Like she was trying to get away from someone...

And she *was*.

Trying to get away from herself.

Because she hated what she'd done.

What you might *have done*, she corrected mentally. *You don't know what you did. It may have been nothing.*

She thought again about the fact that she'd awakened fully dressed.

A good sign...

A *very* good sign.

She decided to believe that she and Jake hadn't done anything.

Well, they had obviously done *something*...

She remembered kissing him.

Making out.

So?

Kissing's fine. What's wrong with kissing? What's wrong with making out?

Nothing...

Unless it led to something else.

And with Jake, it probably hadn't.

Since she was dressed, and everything.

Kim sighed and turned the corner onto West Twelfth Street.

She decided to believe that she and Jake had merely kissed and slept.

That, she could live with....

Even though Jake *was* a jerk who had asked her out, then stood her up.

She decided, as she walked up the sagging steps of her apartment house, to instead forget the whole thing, all of it.

Feeling better already, she headed upstairs to wake Beryl and convince her to go out for a big plate of hash browns.

Chapter 3

"Mom?"

"Kim?"

"Hi!" She switched the phone to her other ear and walked from the kitchen to her room. "I didn't expect you to be home."

"Where else would I be at eleven on a Sunday night?" Suzy asked in her wry way.

"I don't know . . . out on a date with Glenn?"

"Glenn's history."

"Good." Kim hadn't been fond of her mother's latest boyfriend, a bartender at the Upwind Café. "What happened?"

"He was a jerk."

A jerk.

Like Jake.

But Kim didn't want to think about him right now.

"But don't you have to still see him at work and everything?" she asked her mother.

"Yeah, but I'm fine with it. No big deal." She exhaled, and Kim pictured her curled up on the couch in their small living room, smoking a Marlboro and balancing the ashtray on her knee, the way she always did when she talked on the phone.

"How are you doing, Kim?" her mother asked. "Is everything okay?"

No.

"Everything's fine," she lied. "I've been having a blast."

"What did you do all day?"

"Laundry. Finally. But the dryers at the Laundromat wouldn't work, so I had to bring everything home and air dry it in the apartment. And since it's so humid, it's still all wet. I'm sitting here in damp underwear."

Her mother laughed. "Why don't you just put on some dry ones?"

"Because I ran out. Everything's wet. I had to wash every stitch of clothing I own."

"How did you let that happen?" Suzy sounded amused, not critical. She wasn't the kind of mother who kept up with the housework.

"I've been too busy to get to it for the past few weeks," Kim told her.

"Busy with what?"

"Well, there have been tons of parties...."

"What about your classes?"

"What about them?"

"Do you still like them? Are you still doing well?"

"Sure. I'm doing great." Kim changed the subject. "When are you going to come visit?"

"As soon as I can get some time off," Suzy promised. "I'd need at least four or five days, since it's such a trip."

"You could fly."

"Yeah, I could . . . if I won the lottery."

Kim felt a stab of guilt. She knew every penny her mother made was going toward her tuition and rent and books. And Suzy was sending her checks every couple of weeks to cover her expenses so she wouldn't have to get a job while she was at school.

"I don't want you working while you're away at college," her mother had said. "I want you to have time for studying and for fun."

Well, she certainly had spent more than her share on *fun*. Namely, drinks and cigarettes. Somehow, she was always broke well before the next check arrived.

"I can't wait till you come," Kim said brightly now, shoving aside her guilt. "I'll introduce you to everyone and show you around. Maybe we can go to Indianapolis—or even to Chicago. It's only two hours away."

"Really?" Suzy didn't sound thrilled.

Kim realized why.

Her father lived in Chicago.

If you could call him that.

A father was someone who was there in the delivery room when you came into the world, proudly cutting the cord and rocking you in his arms.

A father was in the front row at your school plays, with a video camera, clapping louder than anyone else, even when you messed up your lines.

A father was suspicious of the guys you dated and didn't want you to wear short skirts or tight jeans and made sure you were home by curfew.

Kim had never had a curfew.

Kim had never had a father.

Thomas Kryszka of Chicago was merely a sperm donor, as far as she was concerned.

As far as Suzy was concerned, too.

Her mother had never tried to hide the truth from Kim. She'd always been up front about the fact that she had gotten pregnant, at sixteen, the summer she was a counselor at Camp Timberlake in Pennsylvania. The boy, Tom, was just someone she had dated casually—he was from Chicago and vacationing with his family at a nearby resort.

Suzy hadn't even realized she was pregnant until she went home to Weston Bay that fall. When she'd called Tom to tell him, he'd been nice enough, offering to pay for an abortion.

But Suzy—an only child whose mother was long dead and whose father was a distant workaholic—wanted someone to love.

That was what she'd told Kim.

"I wanted you so badly, sweetie," she'd always said. "I wanted someone to cuddle and take care of and love."

And so she'd had her baby, without Tom's support—but with his knowledge. He hadn't responded to the pictures she'd sent, though according to Suzy, Kim looked just like him. And even later, when he would have been older, a supposedly mature adult, he'd never bothered to find out about his daughter.

Which was fine.

Because Kim hadn't given a damn about him, either.

She had her mother, and Suzy loved her more than enough to make up for not having a father.

She supposed Thomas Kryszka was probably alive and well and living in Chicago—a thought that had crossed her mind, vaguely, since she'd arrived here in the heartland.

But...

So what?

Kim had no intention of looking him up.

And she should have known better than to mention visiting Chicago to her mother. Suzy may not have hidden anything, but that didn't mean she enjoyed talking about Kim's non-father.

"So, Mom," Kim said, anxious to change the subject yet again, "have you seen any of my friends around town?"

"Aren't they all gone?"

"Except Allison. And Grant."

"I've seen Grant. He's home a lot these days, poor kid. I wonder how Karen's doing?" Karen was Grant's mother.

"Not good, according to Bridget the last time I talked to her. And Allison says she looks terrible."

Mrs. Caddaham, unexpectedly widowed at forty, had gone gray overnight. Her husband had dropped dead of a heart attack the very night Grant had graduated from Weston Bay High with Kim and Bridget and the rest of their friends.

It was because of his mother that Grant hadn't gone away to school out West with Bridget, the way they had planned. He couldn't leave his mother alone.

Yet.

Kim knew he was planning on going to Seattle in January, for the spring semester. She just hoped that by then, Karen Caddaham would have picked up the pieces of her life.

It wouldn't have been so bad if the Caddahams hadn't been the sort of couple that was always together, always happy—the kind of parents Kim would have wanted to have, if she'd had *two* parents.

The kind of parents no one she knew seemed to have, except Grant.

His parents had jogged together and gardened together and gone out together every Saturday night, dancing at the Moose lodge. And they were young—not as young as Suzy, who was thirty-three, but younger than most of Kim's friends' parents.

Too young to die.

Kim ached for Grant and his mother. And for Bridget, too. She knew that her friend and Grant were having a terrible time being so far apart, when they were supposed to be away at school together.

They'd been voted Class Couple last year, and Kim fully expected them to finish college, get married, and live happily ever after.

The way Grant's parents should have.

She forced her attention back to the conversation with her mother, who was asking if she needed anything.

"Not a thing, Mom," she said after only a brief hesitation. In truth, she could use some cash, but she knew her mother was struggling to send her what little she could spare.

"You had enough money to pay your share of the phone bill?"

"Yup." She'd given the money to Kevin just last week. The telephone account was in his name.

Each housemate—except Monica, who for some reason had bad credit—had put one of the utilities in their name. The gas was in Kim's, and Kevin had handled paying that, too.

He was in charge of collecting money from everyone and making sure the bills got paid on time. Which was fine with Kim, who knew she would never be able to keep track of who owed what, and which bills were due when.

She had enough trouble remembering her class schedule . . . when she went.

"Are you sure you're all right?" Suzy was asking.

"What do you mean?"

"I don't know . . . you just sound a little . . . quiet."

"I'm fine, Mom."

"Have you met anyone nice to go out with?"

"Anyone nice? No."

Her mother laughed. "Don't tell me the guys at Summervale are losers."

"Not all of them."

Just Jake.

For some reason, she thought again of Joe, the guy from her history class.

He'd said he'd save a seat for her on Monday.

Tomorrow.

Maybe she should go.

But if she went, did it mean she had a thing for Joe?

No. She just thought he was nice. And anyway, she felt guilty for cutting all the time, especially now that she had talked to her mother. She couldn't waste this opportunity for a college education, not when her mother was working so hard to give it to her.

You should go to history tomorrow, she told herself firmly.

But if she did, she wouldn't have her Civil War paper to turn in. And it was too late to start writing one now.

"I know what you mean about guys," Suzy was saying. "I never meet anyone nice myself. But I do have something exciting to tell you about. Remember Gary?"

"Your boss's nephew? The nice, classy, cute guy who doesn't even have an ex-wife?"

"He's the one. Out of the blue he invited me to be his date to a family wedding next weekend."

"You're kidding! Mom, that's great!"

"I know. It's a black-tie reception at some fancy country club on the lake."

"What are you going to wear?"

"I have no idea. But I'm saving up for a new dress. Something fancy."

"Good for you!" Kim felt another stab of guilt, knowing that if it weren't for her, and her college expenses, her mother would have a decent wardrobe instead of living in ripped jeans and outdated shoes.

"I saw a black sequined strapless evening gown in the window of one of those boutiques at the Galleria, and I went in and tried it on. It made me feel so special, Kim."

She smiled. "You *are* special, Mom. You have to buy it."

"You wouldn't believe how much it costs. I almost fell over when I peeked at the price tag. But I've been scrimping, and I'm halfway there," her mother said. "If I can get more hours at the bar this week, I'll have enough to buy it. I've never had an evening gown before. I never even went to my prom," she added ruefully.

Kim thought, *That's because you were home with a colicky baby—me.*

"Buying this dress is going to be a major occasion," Suzy said happily. "I might even treat myself to a manicure before the wedding."

"Or maybe you can have your hair done. It would look great piled on top of your head with little ringlets—"

"A manicure's cheaper," Suzy said with a laugh. "But I'll see what I can do with a curling iron and some bobby pins."

"I wish I could be home to see you all dressed up."

"You just enjoy yourself at school, Kim."

"I will. And Mom, you know what? You don't need to send me my check next week. I've got enough left over from the last one. Put the money toward our dress."

"Kim, I can't do that. I told you I'd send you—"

"Mom, no. I don't need it right now. Really. I want to chip in toward the dress. That way I get to borrow it."

She could practically see her mother grinning. "That's a deal," Suzy said. "I love you."

"I love you, too."

"Study hard."

"I will."

I swear I'll start. And I'll even go to class . . . and I promise I won't fail history.

She said a quick goodbye to her mother and hung up, then looked around for the scrap of paper where she'd scribbled all her hometown friends' new phone numbers.

She couldn't find it.

Well, Allison would have Zara's number.

She started to dial the DeMitris' house, then realized it was way too late to be calling them. Allison's parents freaked out if the phone rang after nine o'clock.

She considered phoning Zara's parents, who were probably still up, but decided against it. Mr. and Mrs. Benjamin made her uncomfortable. For one thing, they were so smart, both professors at the local state university. Kim was always afraid she was going to open her mouth and sound like an idiot in front of them.

For another thing, they always seemed so stiff and slightly disapproving of her, as though they expected her to corrupt their daughter.

Lord knew, Kim had tried.

In her opinion, Zara desperately needed to loosen up. But even at parties, Zara had always managed to hold herself apart from the action, as responsible and quiet as always.

Maybe college had changed her, Kim thought. Maybe she'd even lend Kim the history paper she supposedly couldn't find.

Zara was the most organized person Kim had ever met. She probably had every school assignment she'd ever done, neatly labeled and organized in an alphabetical file. There was no way Zara had lost the paper.

She just didn't want Kim to borrow it. She probably thought Kim was going to put her own name on it and hand it in.

Which was exactly what she had in mind.

She didn't love the idea of cheating, but she hadn't realized the history paper was due until it was too late to write one. And she couldn't start now, a week later.

No, there was nothing to do but beg Zara to loan her the paper, just this once.

Cameron would have Zara's number at Dannon College. All she had to do was get Cameron's number.

You really should get organized, Kim told herself. It was

pretty bad that she couldn't even keep track of her friends' new phone numbers.

She dialed the Colliers' number back in Weston Bay. Cameron's parents would be up, and they were laid back enough not to care about a late-night phone call.

Mrs. Collier answered, and sounded happy to hear from Kim. "How do you like Summervale?" she asked pleasantly, after giving Kim Cameron's phone number at school in Florida.

"It's a lot of fun. It feels like I've been here forever."

"Cameron says the same thing about being in Florida."

Mrs. Collier said they were going down to visit Cameron over Thanksgiving next month, and Kim told her that she and some of her friends were going to Florida for Spring Break.

"You'll have to visit Cameron," Mrs. Collier said.

"Actually, we were planning on staying with her," Kim said. "If she has room."

"I'm sure she'll make room. She'll be thrilled to have you visit. She'll be living in the sorority house by then. Are you joining a sorority, Kim?"

"No, I'm not." Summervale was a big Greek school, and she had considered rushing...for about a minute. Then she'd decided it was way too complicated, and she'd much rather skip the hassle and have fun. You didn't have to be in a sorority to go to the big frat parties.

"Well, anyway," Mrs. Collier went on, "when you visit Cameron in Florida, you'll be able to meet Tad."

"Oh, right." Kim knew her friend was seriously dating someone she'd met at school.

Lucky Cameron, to have met someone decent.

She hung up with Mrs. Collier and dialed Cameron's number. Her roommate, Shanta, answered and told her Cameron was out.

"With that guy, Tad?" Kim asked.

"I think so."

Lucky Cameron, Kim thought again after hanging up.

Her friend always seemed to get the best of everything.

Her parents were great. Her mother, a photographer, traveled a lot, and sometimes Cameron and her two sisters went with her. They'd been everywhere, including Europe. And Cameron's father was a doctor, so they had a lot of money.

The Colliers' house was in upscale Maplebridge Heights, not far from Finch Street in distance, but a world away when it came to class. The Colliers had an in-ground pool and a Jacuzzi, and their house—including Cameron's room—was professionally decorated.

Cameron was gorgeous and fun and nice—one of the most popular girls in their class at Weston Bay. Everyone loved her—including teachers and guys.

Now here she was going to college in sunny Florida, pledging the sorority of her choice, with a terrific new boyfriend.

If she wasn't one of my best friends, I'd hate her guts, Kim decided, hanging up the phone and imagining Cameron and that Tad guy having a romantic evening on some moonlit beach.

Meanwhile, here I am, sitting here in wet underwear trying to scam Zara's history paper and having no clue whether or not I slept with Jake the Jerk last night.

Sometimes, Kim decided, life just wasn't fair.

Kim hesitated in the doorway of the enormous lecture hall, looking around for Joe.

How was she supposed to find him in this crowd scene?

Well, at least she didn't have to worry that the professor was going to zero in on her and ask her for the missing paper. There had to be at least a hundred and fifty people in this class.

Kim considered leaving, since she didn't see Joe and since she wasn't in the mood to listen to a boring history lecture this early on a Monday morning in the first place.

But then she heard someone calling her name behind her, and turned to see a familiar lanky figure hurrying toward her.

"You beat me here," Joe said, grinning his white, toothy grin.

"Yeah, I guess I did."

He looked pleased.

Did he assume it was because she was anxious to see him or something? She didn't want him to think that.

He wasn't her type.

Still, he was nice. And nice guys seemed to be few and far between here at Summervale.

And anyway, it was about time she'd decided to come to history class. She couldn't just skip all her classes, all the time.

"Where do you want to sit?" Joe asked.

"In back," she answered promptly. No need to tempt fate by plunking down right in front of the professor.

"I usually sit in front."

Of course you do, Kim thought. She shrugged and said, "You can go ahead if you want, but I'm staying back here. I have to."

"Why?"

"Because I'm . . . nearsighted."

Wasn't nearsighted the thing where you couldn't see things close up?

Or was it the other way around? Was that farsighted?

Since Joe wasn't arguing, he must not know the difference. And there was no way for him to tell that she had twenty-twenty vision, either.

They made their way to two vacant seats in the second-to-last row. Joe made small talk as they waited the few minutes for class to start. Then the professor, a no-nonsense-type woman named Dr. Viveca Armstrong, showed up and plunged right into a lecture about Andrew Johnson's impeachment.

Somehow, Kim thought, sitting here shoulder-to-shoulder next to Joe seemed very intimate. Even though they were in public, both fully clothed and staring straight ahead at the professor.

She could hear Joe breathing, could smell his musky soap scent, could feel the subtle vibrations of his foot that was just barely tapping a faint rhythm on the floor beside her chair.

And she realized, as Dr. Armstrong droned on up front,

that she was wondering what it would be like to be even closer to Joe.

As in, kissing him.

The thought made her face flush.

She glanced his way out of the corner of her eye, hoping he couldn't somehow sense what she was thinking.

She had to stop this.

She didn't want to have a crush on this guy, with his neatly tabbed three-ring binder and his unscuffed white sneakers.

Someone like Joe wouldn't be any fun at all.

He'd probably think Kim was wild.

Guys like Joe always did.

Guys like Joe, Nice Guys, always made her feel like a Bad Girl.

He probably didn't drink, or go to frat parties.

And she knew he wouldn't like a girl who smoked.

Kim wasn't about to give up her Salems.

And the last thing she wanted was to spend her college life tied down in a relationship with some stick-in-the mud Mr. Nice Guy who disapproved of her.

Right?

Right.

After class Joe followed her out into the corridor.

"Did you hand in your paper yet?" he asked.

She spun around. "Did you see me hand in my paper?"

He looked flustered. "Uh, no."

God, she hated herself. What had he done to deserve her snapping?

"I got an extension, remember?" she said more gently, to fix it.

"Yeah, I remember."

It was too late. He looked miffed.

He checked his watch and said, "I've got to go. I have another class in ten minutes over in Spidell Hall."

"Okay, see you on Wednesday."

He looked surprised. "You're coming to class on Wednesday?"

What had made her say that? She had no intention of regularly showing up for History 101, or any other course that didn't have required attendance.

Hadn't she said as much to Beryl just this morning?

But to Joe she said, "Sure, why not?"

"Okay, see you Wednesday then," he told her with a shrug and a wave.

She watched him walk away for a moment, noticing that his butt looked pretty good in those black corduroys he was wearing.

Then she tossed her French braid and headed in the opposite direction, toward home.

"**Want** to go to Chicago this weekend?" Beryl asked idly as she painted Kim's pinky nail a bright red.

"Chicago? What for?"

"I don't know. It's only a few hours away. And anyway, I just feel bored." Beryl, who was lying on her stomach on Kim's bed as she painted her nails, bent her long legs and waved her feet in the air behind her. "I want to do something different."

"Well, it's only Monday night," Kim pointed out. "You've got four more boring days ahead of you before the weekend, no matter what."

"I know, but if I have something to look forward to, the week'll go by faster."

"No—if you have something to look forward to, the week'll drag by," Kim said. "Like when you're a kid, and Christmas Eve seems like the longest day of the year because all you want to do is go to bed and wake up and see that Santa came."

"We didn't do Santa at my house," said Beryl, who, like Kim, had been raised by a single mother.

But Beryl had an older sister, and Beryl's mother was nothing like Suzy. Candace Starmeyer was overweight and middle-aged and intellectual. Not to mention totally conservative. She'd be shocked at most of the things Beryl said and did, but of course, she had no idea. Beryl was always joking that her mother thought she was Miss Perfect.

"You're kidding," Kim said, looking up at her friend in dismay. "Why didn't you have Santa?"

"You know my mother. She's the original Scrooge. And besides, she didn't believe in creating unrealistic fairy tales."

"That's really cruel, to deprive you of Santa. I mean, it's on the level with child abuse, you know?"

"Tell me about it. Even though she said there was no such

thing, I believed in him anyway. I went halfway through grade school wondering why my house was the only one on the block that he skipped every year. I mean, I was no angel, but I never thought I'd been all *that* bad."

"I can't believe we've been friends forever and I never knew this about you."

"I never told anyone. I was too ashamed."

"God, Beryl, this is so sad. I feel like I should hug you or something."

"Yeah, well, don't. I'm almost finished with this last nail, and I don't want you messing it up. What do you think?"

Kim surveyed her fresh manicure. "You know, I think I liked the coral polish better after all."

Beryl's head snapped up and she had a killer expression in her eyes.

Kim laughed. "Just kidding."

"You better be, because I'm not stripping all ten nails *again*."

"I won't make you. Anyway, about Chicago..." Kim's mind wandered back. "What did you have in mind?"

Beryl shrugged. "We could go to a club, dancing, or something. Hang out on Rush Street."

"Yeah, I guess."

"Why don't you look thrilled? Aren't you as bored as I am? Isn't that why you suggested getting a manicure tonight in the first place?"

"It is, but...maybe we can go to Indianapolis instead."

Beryl made a face. "Why? Chicago's way bigger, and way better, and not that much farther away. What do you have against it?"

"My father lives there."

It had slipped out before Kim realized what she was saying.

Beryl looked up at her, startled. "Your *father*? I thought you didn't have a father."

"Now, Beryl," Kim said in a mock patronizing tone, "weren't you paying attention in seventh grade health class?"

"What I mean is, I thought you didn't know anything about him, except that he was some teenager who knocked your mother up in passing."

"That's exactly what I know about him. That, and that he lives in Chicago. *Lived* in Chicago," she amended. "For all I know, he could be dead now."

"Why? How old can he be?"

"I guess he's like, my mother's age. But that doesn't mean he's still alive."

"Well, don't you want to find out?"

"No!" she said so vehemently that she almost knocked the polish bottle out of Beryl's hand.

"Careful... Why not? Aren't you curious? If I didn't know my own father was a total asshole, having spent six miserable years living under the same roof with him before the divorce, I'd be curious."

"Why would I want to know anything about someone who has no interest in knowing anything about me?"

"How do you know that?"

"My mother told me, remember?"

Kim had told Beryl her life story—well, most of it— enough times over the years. In fact, Beryl knew more about her past than Allison and Cameron and Bridget and Zara did. They all had "normal" families, and Kim never got the feeling that they understood or accepted her situation as readily as Beryl had.

"Listen, Kim, I know you and Suzy are totally close, but maybe you shouldn't take everything she says as gospel."

"What's that supposed to mean?"

"She's a bitter unwed mother—"

"Beryl!"

"Kim, I'm just stating the facts. Why would your mother have anything good to say about the guy who knocked her up when she was fifteen?"

"Sixteen. And if he was so great, where is he?" Kim shot back. "Why wouldn't he want to be there for her? For *me*?"

"How do you know he didn't want to?"

"Because he wasn't!"

"How do you know he knew about you in the first place?"

"Because my mother told me he did!"

Beryl just looked at her.

And then it dawned on her.

Of all the times she'd rehashed her mother's version of her birth, how was it that she'd never realized that it was just that . . . *her mother's version*?

What if her mother didn't remember all the facts exactly as they'd happened?

Or...

What if her mother had twisted things a little?

"Are you saying," she asked Beryl slowly, "that my mother might have lied to me about telling my father?"

"I'm not saying anything either way. I just wonder if you ever considered that Suzy might have...omitted some details."

"You think my father never knew about me in the first place!"

"Kim! I do not!" Beryl peered at her. "Do *you* think that?"

"No!"

But a pinprick of doubt had taken hold deep inside of her.

What if Suzy really hadn't told her the whole truth?

What if she'd never really contacted Thomas Kryszka and told him she was pregnant?

But why wouldn't she?

Kim's thoughts tripped over each other, scrambling to create some kind of order from emotional chaos.

Okay, how about this...

What if Suzy had been afraid, as a young, pregnant teenager, that he would somehow try to take her baby away from her?

After all, poor lonely Suzy had been so desperate for a baby to love. Would she really have taken a chance and revealed to a semi-stranger that she was pregnant with his child?

Every day lately, it seemed, you heard about birth parents who tried to get their children back.

Kim wondered if her mother had feared that might happen

with Thomas Kryszka. He had been wealthy, she knew—at least, his parents had been. Wealth meant power.

And Suzy hadn't had a mother who would stand by her to offer her support—and make sure she did the right thing.

Kim knew that her grandfather, who had remarried and retired to Arizona a few years back, hadn't been thrilled when his only daughter became pregnant at sixteen. Still, he'd done his best to help Suzy financially, even though he'd been laid off from his job a year after Kim was born.

Wouldn't he have made sure his daughter had notified the father of her baby, even if Suzy hadn't wanted to?

"You have this really weird look on your face, Kim."

Beryl's voice broke into her thoughts, and she forced her attention back, focusing on her friend's concerned brown eyes.

"I was just thinking..."

"About your father."

"Yeah."

"Look, Kim, I don't want you to start getting all kinds of crazy ideas about how he's out there somewhere, pining away, wishing he had a daughter just like you. Because chances are, your mother's telling the truth, and she told him about you years ago, and he was some jerk guy, like Jake and everyone else we know, and he just didn't give a damn."

Kim considered that. It made a lot of sense.

But then again...

"There's a chance that he didn't know," she told Beryl. "I

mean, you're right. All I have is my mother's word that she told him about me. Maybe she just wanted me to forget about him. Case closed."

"Right."

"But why would she do that? Why wouldn't she want me to have a father?"

"The same reason my mother gets all pissed off whenever my sister and I do our duty and visit good old dad at his condo. Because he burned her. And she's bitter."

"Your dad had an affair on your mom, Beryl. My mother barely knew my dad."

My dad . . .

The phrase sounded so strange coming from her mouth, and she realized she'd never in her life uttered it before.

My dad.

She'd never, ever considered that she might somehow actually *have* a dad someday.

Thomas Kryszka was written off for good, as far as Kim was concerned.

Until now.

Now, she couldn't help wondering . . .

"Why don't you ask her?" Beryl suggested.

"Ask my mother? If she lied about him? No way," Kim said.

"Why not?"

"Because if she didn't, she'd be really hurt that I'd even think such a thing. I've always totally trusted her."

"And if she *did* . . . ?"

"If she *did*," Kim paused, trying to imagine that unlikely scenario, "then she probably wouldn't tell me the truth about it *now*, after all these years."

"She might if you asked her."

"Well, I can't ask her," Kim said firmly, and looked down at her hand. "Are you done?"

"With the manicure?" Beryl shrugged. "I guess. But—"

"Good," Kim said in a case-closed tone, and turned away.

Chapter 4

"Zara?"

"Yes? Kim?" Recognition infiltrated Zara's voice, along with surprise.

"I know, you're shocked to hear from me. I'm really bad about keeping in touch," Kim said nervously.

She wasn't looking forward to asking her friend about that history paper again, and wondered if she could pass this off as a totally social phone call, then casually bring up the paper at the end.

"How's everything?" she asked Zara.

"Busy. I've got a huge history paper due tomorrow."

"Speaking of history papers," Kim said after only a moment's hesitation, "I don't suppose you've found that one on the Reconstruction that you wrote last year? I thought you could E-mail it to me."

There was a moment of silence.

Then Zara said, "Didn't you get my E-mail about that?"

"Oh, right, I did. You said you lost it. But I E-mailed you back, thinking you might have found it by now."

Zara didn't say whether she'd received Kim's latest E-mail, and Kim didn't want to ask.

Instead she said lamely, "I guess you haven't found it?"

More silence.

Kim fumbled awkwardly for something to say.

Zara beat her to it, though.

"Kim," she said, clearing her throat, "I really don't want to give you that paper."

Stunned, Kim felt her mouth drop open.

She couldn't think of a thing to say.

Never in a million years had she expected Zara to come right out and say she didn't want to hand it over.

Excuses, she could handle. But blunt honesty?

She suddenly felt about as big as her newly polished pinky nail.

"I know you're going to put your name on it and pass it off as your own," Zara went on, her voice wavering only slightly, "and I just don't want to be a part of something like that."

"I wasn't going to steal it," Kim protested, finding her voice and forcing it out. "I just wanted to read it. To get ideas."

Zara paused, then said, "Are you sure?"

Kim frowned. "Sure I'm sure."

A beat.

"Did you find it, Zara?"

"No."

"Oh." Kim knew Zara was lying, and found herself annoyed until she realized she was lying, too, about her intent for borrowing the paper.

"Well..." She tried to think of a way out of the hole she'd somehow stumbled into. "How's your roommate?"

"I don't have one anymore," Zara said, sounding relieved at the chance to change the subject.

Lord knew Kim was an expert at that.

"Really? What happened?" Kim asked, even though she remembered that Allison had told her Zara's roommate was a psycho or something.

"She and I were total opposites," Zara told her. "She was constantly on the phone, making noise, smoking..."

"Sounds kind of like me," Kim said wryly, and heard Zara laugh.

"I wish," her friend said. "If she was like you, at least she'd be likable. Clarice wasn't."

Kim felt a flicker of warmth at Zara's compliment. Of all her friends, Zara was the most different from her; the one she couldn't really relate to—particularly as they got older and grew in opposite directions.

But, Kim realized, twelve years of shared experiences didn't vanish just like that, even now that their lives had taken them a thousand miles apart. She felt bonded to Zara Benjamin in a way that she didn't feel with the new friends she'd made at Summervale—people she saw every day; people who had a lot more in common with her on the surface.

She and Zara spent a few minutes catching up on their mutual friends.

And before they hung up, Zara apologized for not loaning Kim her paper. "I just can't do it," she said in a totally un-Zara-like, straightforward way.

"I understand," Kim said lightly, wondering what had happened to transform Zara from a wimp to *this*.

"I'm really sorry, Kim...."

"It's no big deal."

But it was.

She hung up and sat there with the phone in hand, brooding.

Tomorrow, Wednesday, was history class again.

What would happen if she didn't hand in that paper? Would she fail the course?

Her other four classes were under control. She was caught up on her assignments for English comp, had taken and passed the anthropology quizzes, and even attended her two other courses regularly. Intro to communications because it was fun, and basic algebra because she had to; the instructor took attendance.

Then there was history.

It was too late in the semester to drop the course and add something else in its place.

And failing would mean she'd either have to take an extra

class next semester, or go to summer school to make up the credits.

That would cost money.

Kim thought of her mother, and she knew she couldn't let that happen.

She had to get her butt to class tomorrow, and she had to talk to Dr. Armstrong about the paper.

Kim hadn't planned on sitting with Joe in history class.

But she was distracted when she walked into the room, thinking about her looming confrontation with the instructor. She didn't remember that she'd decided to avoid Joe until she'd practically crashed into him.

How could she miss? He was standing right in the aisle, as if he were waiting for someone.

"Hi, Kim," he said, looking friendly but not overly so.

"Hi."

"I saved you a seat." He gestured to the spot where they had sat on Monday, and she saw that Joe had put a three-ring binder on each desk.

No one she knew carried three-ring binders, she thought, inexplicably irritated. Everyone used spiral bound notebooks to take notes. A few people even used yellow legal pads.

Didn't Joe know that? Was he oblivious to what was going on around him?

They sat, and Kim stared moodily at the empty podium in

front of the room. A few students were milling around, waiting to catch the instructor before she started the lecture.

Kim wouldn't approach Dr. Armstrong until after class. She
didn't want anyone overhearing what she had to say.

Which was...?

She had no idea what to tell the professor about why
her paper wasn't in yet. In high school this type of thing had
come naturally. By senior year at Weston Bay, she had been
famous—notorious, really—for her elaborate excuses. Some
of the teachers had found them amusing; others had grown
weary of her inventive reasons why her homework wasn't
done or why she hadn't been in class the day before. But at
least all of them knew her, and none of them, in the end, had
failed her.

College was different.

Dr. Viveca Armstrong didn't know Kim from the girl sitting
next to her, and she wasn't going to cut her any slack.

Kim thought of Zara, and how she had been truthful last
night when she'd said she didn't want to loan her the paper.

Maybe honesty was the route to go with Dr. Armstrong.

Maybe she should just march up to her, say that she hadn't
done the paper because...

Well, because she'd been lazy and hadn't felt like bothering,
and besides, she was a born procrastinator.

Maybe Dr. Armstrong would straighten her glasses on her
nose, and crack a smile, and say that Kim's honesty was refresh-
ing and she wished all her students had such candid integrity.

Yeah, right.

"So what have you been up to?" Joe asked, at her elbow, startling her.

"Not much," she said briefly. "How about you?"

"Working. Studying. And I'm on the soccer team."

That figured. She should have known Mr. All-American would be well rounded.

"That's nice."

"Hey, you aren't by any chance looking for a part-time job, are you?"

"Me? No. Why?"

"Because a buddy of mine is quitting the record store. He's giving notice tomorrow."

"Well, I don't need a job," Kim told him again.

She kept an eye on the door at the front of the room, waiting for Dr. Armstrong to appear. She might be able to tell, just by looking at her, what kind of mood she was in today. Then she could figure out how to word what she had to say.

She should have prepared herself for this last night, but Beryl had come home with a bottle of Jamaican rum she'd won playing cards at Gregg and Phil's, and they'd sat up drinking it with pineapple juice until three A.M.

Headaches were so much a part of Kim's routine existence now that she'd barely noticed her pounding skull this morning. But she'd been utterly exhausted, and the last thing she wanted to do was drag herself out of bed for class.

But you did it anyway, she congratulated herself. *You made it here, and now you have to go through with your little talk with Dr. Armstrong.*

"What are you doing Friday night?" Joe was asking now.

Startled, she turned toward him. He was going to ask her out? Didn't he get the hint, that she wasn't interested?

Well, okay, that wasn't exactly true.

She might be attracted to him....

But that didn't mean she wanted a romance.

"Why?" she asked, formulating an excuse in her head.

"Because our soccer team's playing at home," he said. "You should go to the game. We need all the spectators we can get, because the university's thinking of cutting the soccer program next year, when they adjust the budget."

She stared at him.

He wasn't asking her out?

He just wanted her to show up and help save his soccer team from being sent into oblivion?

"Unfortunately, I can't help you out, Joe. I'm going to Chicago with my housemate."

"Oh, well, maybe next time. I'll get a schedule of our home games for you."

Dr. Armstrong had appeared at the front of the room.

Kim's mind was so busy digesting the fact that Joe hadn't asked her out that she forgot to evaluate the instructor's mood.

Maybe Joe wasn't interested in her after all.

Maybe he merely wanted to be friends.

Nothing wrong with that, Kim reminded herself. *It's what you wanted, too.*

Wasn't it?

Sure it was.

But *why* wasn't he interested in her?

Maybe because he didn't think she was good enough for him. He was a Scarsdale-born jock with brains and bucks. He probably thought she was some hard-drinking, fast-living tramp from the wrong side of the tracks.

God, you sound like a trailer for some cheesy teen romance movie.

But it was the truth.

And even if she'd had no intention of going out with Joe, it would have been nice if he'd at least asked.

Well, Kim didn't have time to bother worrying about what Joe thought of her.

She flipped her spiral-bound notebook open as Dr. Armstrong began today's lecture.

She took notes, and she paid attention, and by the end of class, she was startled to find that not only had she learned something about politics in the eighteen-sixties, but she'd actually enjoyed it.

"Which way are you headed?" Joe asked as they stood when class was over.

"I have to talk to Dr. Armstrong," Kim told him, and gave a casual wave. "I'll see you later."

Was it her imagination, or did he look a little disappointed?

Of course it's your imagination, she told herself, and headed down the sloping steps to the front of the lecture hall.

Dr. Armstrong was apparently trying to shake off an earnest, bespectacled guy who was rhapsodizing about the corruption in Ulysses S. Grant's cabinet.

"Yes? Can I help you?" she asked Kim finally, after dismissing the guy with a polite but firm "See you on Friday."

"Um, Dr. Armstrong..." Kim began, and hesitated.

"Yes?" The woman peered at her over her dark-framed glasses, and Kim was startled to see that her eyes were unexpectedly pretty, a warm, honeyed hazel color. They seemed out of place in a face that was all stern, sharp lines, framed by graying hair pulled back severely in a plain black clip.

"I'm Kim Garfield."

The woman nodded expectantly, showing not a flicker of recognition.

"I wanted to talk to you about my paper...."

"I've posted the grades outside my office door," Dr. Armstrong said dismissively. "I'll be handing them back next week."

"I know, but my paper..." Kim hesitated, clearing her throat. "I didn't see my grade posted."

Now where had *that* come from?

Not only hadn't she seen the listing of posted grades—not only had she never set *foot* near Dr. Armstrong's office!—but she hadn't handed in a paper in the first place. So how could she have seen her grade posted?

"Excuse me?" Dr. Armstrong said.

"I didn't see my grade," Kim said again. "I thought that maybe you—maybe my paper had gotten lost."

Yes, that sounded less accusatory than *maybe you lost my paper.*

Dr. Armstrong blinked. "You handed it in with the others in class last week?"

"No, I was sick that morning—food poisoning," she elaborated. "But I dropped it off in your mailbox near your office that night, the way you said we should if we weren't going to be in class when an assignment is due."

That much, she remembered reading on the syllabus Dr. Armstrong had handed out the first day.

"I see." The professor was studying her, as if trying to discern whether she was telling the truth. "And what was the topic of your paper?"

"The impact of Reconstruction on the freed slaves," she said, arbitrarily picking a topic she'd seen somewhere in her text.

"I assume you kept a copy of your paper on file?"

Uh-oh. "No, actually, I didn't. My computer was on the blink, so I typed it on my, uh, father's old manual typewriter."

Your father's *old typewriter? You don't even have a father!*

Dr. Armstrong appeared to be digesting all this. "You must still have your notes and research handy," she said finally, looking Kim in the eye.

Don't push your luck, Kim.

"Yes, I do. . . ."

"Good. Then it won't be too troublesome for you to rewrite the paper for me."

"It . . . no. It won't."

"I'll give you until Monday morning," Dr. Armstrong said, still watching her carefully. "But no later."

"Thank you," Kim said, afraid to add anything else.

She turned to go.

"And Ms. Garfield?"

"Yes?"

"In the future, you would be wise to either repair your computer and save your work on disk, or invest a dollar or two in a photocopy of your finished paper."

"I definitely will," Kim promised, and hurried out of the room.

It wasn't until she was outside on the sidewalk that led to the Student Union that she let out an enormous sigh of relief.

You did it! she thought exultantly, and grinned at the sunny October day.

But as she hurried along in the throng of students, she found that she wasn't quite as exhilarated as she should be.

You lied. You decided you weren't going to, and then you did it anyway.

Well, if she'd told Dr. Armstrong the truth, she wouldn't have this second chance to turn in her paper. She'd probably have a failing grade, and then she'd fail the course, and then she'd be wasting her poor mother's hard-earned money.

No, she'd done what she had to do.

For Suzy's sake, she told herself.

And for her own.

And it wasn't like she was going to plagiarize someone else's paper.

No, she was going to write one of her own....

And she was going to work harder than she'd ever worked before in her life, just to prove she wasn't a loser.

Starting tonight.

No...

Starting tomorrow.

Tonight, she remembered, was the Sigma Kappas' Harvest Moon party. She couldn't miss that—it was all anyone had talked about all week, one of the biggest parties of the semester.

Okay, maybe your priorities are in the wrong place, she told herself, feeling guiltier with every step she took.

What she *should* do was skip the party and spend the night at the library, working on her paper.

But what she *would* do, instead, was go to the library *before* the party.

That way she wouldn't miss out on anything fun.

"I can't believe this," Kim said, raking a hand through her hair.

"Calm down," Beryl said for the hundredth time in the last hour.

"Calm down? I'm *dead*, Beryl. My bookbag has vanished into thin air." She paced across the living room and back again to the kitchen, where Beryl was sitting cross-legged at the table, eating from a bag of Baked Lays Potato Chips.

"No, it hasn't vanished," she told Kim. "It's not magical. You must have left it at the library."

"I told you, I didn't. I remember bringing it with me to the party. I was all irritated because I was thinking that now I'd have to carry it around all night."

"Well, obviously you didn't carry it around. You set it down somewhere."

"I just finished combing the entire frat house from top to bottom, Beryl."

And that certainly hadn't been a pleasant task the day after a huge party. Every surface in the Sigma Kappa house was sticky, and the place reeked of stale smoke and beer. Most of the brothers were disgruntled at being disturbed, and she'd made an enemy or two when she'd insisted on knocking on closed doors in her quest for her missing bookbag.

"It just wasn't there," Kim said. "Someone must have stolen it."

"Who'd steal a bag full of books?"

"My Walkman was in there, and a couple of tapes. And some money."

"How much?"

"All I had to my name. About eight bucks."

"You should call the library," Beryl advised. "Maybe you're wrong about bringing it with you to the party. You were to-tally wasted last night."

"But I was sober when I got there!" Kim protested. "I re-member bringing my bag."

Beryl silently handed her the cordless phone. "Call. Just to make sure."

"Fine." Kim looked up the number and dialed, grumbling the whole time that she knew the bag wasn't going to turn up.

Sure enough, the librarian told her that no, they hadn't found a missing bookbag, and yes, they would have come across it this morning if it were there.

Hanging up, Kim glared at Beryl. "Satisfied?"

Beryl shrugged. "It'll turn up."

"God, when? I spent five hours researching the Reconstruction Era last night before I went to the party. All my notes were in that bag. Now I have to start again from scratch. And ... Oh, my God!"

She clapped a hand to her mouth.

"What?" Beryl asked, looking concerned.

"My books! What about my books? They were in the bag."

"Not *all* of them."

Kim nodded miserably. "I figured since I was going to the library, I might as well be ambitious and study for all my classes. I had no idea the stupid paper research was going to take so long," she clarified, when Beryl shot her an incredulous look. "I figured I'd get that out of the way, then kill five birds with one stone ... what?"

"What, what?"

"Why are you looking at me like that?"

"Like what?"

"Like I'm crazy," Kim said.

"Because sometimes I think you are. You don't crack a book for almost two months, and then you're suddenly lugging every text you own to the library."

"I guess I panicked. I felt like I was in danger of falling behind. Now what am I supposed to do?"

"You'll have to write off the bookbag," Beryl said matter-of-factly.

"But it was a graduation gift from my grandfather—"

"And replace your books."

"Do you know how much I spent on them?"

"I know. Hundreds."

"Where am I supposed to get that kind of money to replace them? All I had left was eight dollars, and now that's gone, too."

"I wish I could loan you some money," Beryl said, "but I'm flat broke, too. I think it's time to hit up dear old dad for another fat check."

Kim knew Beryl was an expert at getting her absent father to feel guilty and toss cash her way every now and then. All she had to do was pick up the phone, whine a little, and the money was hers.

"Isn't your mother sending you a check every week or two?" Beryl asked Kim.

"Yeah, but only enough to live on." Not that the amount Suzy sent wasn't generous, in the grand scheme of things—but somehow, it never seemed to go far enough.

And the thought of just how much of that "living" money she'd been spending on beer and cigarettes and cover charges at parties made Kim feel slightly ill.

"You'll just have to tell her what happened and ask her for more money to replace the books."

"I can't."

"Why not?"

"First of all, what am I supposed to do, say that I got drunk and lost track of my bag?"

"Tell her it was stolen."

Kim bristled. "I don't want to lie."

Beryl gave her a level look, as if to say, *since when?*

"And besides," Kim went on, "I can't ask her for the money. She's working two jobs just to keep me here. I'm draining her dry."

"She must have some money set aside for emergencies," Beryl pointed out.

Kim thought of the black tie wedding and the dress Suzy hoped to buy.

If her mother knew she needed money to replace her books, she'd hand over her evening gown fund in a moment.

She'd probably even joke about it, saying she wasn't cut out for black sequins, anyway.

Her mother had always come through for her somehow when she needed money. Always. Even when it seemed there wasn't a dime to spare.

For a moment Kim considered calling Suzy right now. That way she wouldn't have to spend another minute worrying about how she was going to replace the books.

But she couldn't do that, she realized. Not this time.

This time Kim was going to bail herself out of her own mess. She just didn't have the faintest idea how.

•   •   •

"Kim!"

"Hi, Joe."

"I thought that was you." He set down the box of CDs he'd been unpacking over by the side wall and walked over to the counter at the front of the store, where she had hovered since walking in a minute ago.

"It's me, all right," she said brightly. "You just didn't recognize me because I'm not wearing jeans for the first time in, like, a month."

"You look nice," he said, glancing at her outfit.

She felt conspicuous in her long black skirt and matching blazer. She was even wearing nylons, and had borrowed a pair of dress pumps from Monica. They were a half-size too small, and she'd limped the last two blocks, trying not to think about the monster blisters she'd have by tonight.

"Thanks. Are you the only one working?" she asked Joe.

"No. My boss, Vince, is out back. What's up?"

"I just...I remembered that you said there might be a job opening here?"

"There is. Vince just called the paper to place a want ad this morning."

"Well, I was thinking that maybe he could hire me." Kim forced herself to look Joe in the eye.

"I thought you didn't need a job."

"I do now."

She didn't bother to explain, and Joe didn't ask. He just said, "I'll get Vince."

"Thanks."

She thrummed the countertop with her fingers nervously as she waited, glancing around the place.

It was small, but every inch of space was filled with inventory. There was a big classical section in back, and a whole wall devoted to jazz.

Kim's music tastes ran mostly to alternative, although she knew quite a bit about folk and bluegrass, thanks to Suzy. But when it came to everything else, she was pretty much in the dark.

There was no way Vince was going to hire her.

This was a totally dumb idea, she scolded herself.

But what other choice did she have?

She needed money, fast. And the only way to get it—the only *legal* way—was by working to earn it.

She'd figured the music store was her best bet, since Joe had told her they were looking for someone.

She didn't want to spend time combing the classifieds or putting her application in at fast-food restaurants—a heinous thought—unless she absolutely had to.

Of course, she wasn't crazy about the idea of working alongside Joe, either.

At least, that was what she kept telling herself.

Well, she probably didn't have to worry, because she wasn't going to get this job. She didn't know enough about music.

The door at the back of the store swung open and Joe

reemerged, followed by a stocky, bearded man wearing a shirt and tie with a pair of jeans.

The two of them started for the counter, but Joe was way-laid by a browser with a question.

"You must be Kim," Joe's boss said, reaching her and shaking her hand. "I'm Vince Frederick, the manager of Tambourine Man."

"It's nice to meet you."

"Joe says you're looking for part-time work?"

"Yes."

"Have you ever operated a cash register?"

She nodded. "I worked at the Gap last Christmas. If you need a reference I can—"

"Do you know anything about music?"

She nodded again and cleared her throat, wondering if he was planning to interview her right here and now. "I, uh, like all kinds of music. Alternative's my favorite, but I also like rock… and folk and bluegrass. And, uh, I've been getting into jazz lately."

Major lie.

"And classical," she added for good measure.

He just nodded, either unimpressed or uninterested. "Okay, when would you be able to start?"

She blinked. "Right away?"

"Good. You free to stay tonight for training?"

"Tonight?" She had been planning to get home in time to catch the new episode of *Survivor.* She and her housemates played a drinking game every Thursday night while watching TV.

"Tonight would be fine," she told Vince Frederick. "Uh... don't you need references or anything?"

"Nah. Joey says he knows you, and he said I should hire you. I got all guys working here, anyway. We could use a pretty babe or two, to attract customers."

She flushed, wondering if this qualified as sexual harassment.

Not that she was going to do anything about it if it did. She needed this job.

She actually *had* this job.

She couldn't believe it had been so simple.

"Okay, Joe," Vince said as Joe made his way back to the counter. "She's all set. You can train her tonight."

Joe grinned. "Great."

"Great," she echoed, and pasted on a bright I'm-so-happy-to-be-here smile.

Chapter 5

Friday morning Kim got up for history class.

She figured she might as well go, not just because it would look good for Dr. Armstrong's benefit, but because Joe would be there.

She'd been surprised to discover, last night at the store, that he wasn't as straitlaced as she'd expected. He had a good sense of humor and made her laugh when he mimicked a pretentious customer after she'd left the store.

And he liked a lot of the same music she did—Coldplay and Alanis were his favorites, too.

He'd been very complimentary about her clerking skills, too, telling her he couldn't believe how quickly she'd caught on, and that it had taken him a lot longer to get the hang of the inventory system.

When they'd said good night, he'd added, "I'll see you to-morrow in class."

And Kim had repeated, "See you tomorrow."

So here she was, gulping down a cup of instant coffee in the cluttered kitchen of her apartment before she got ready to leave for campus.

She'd only had three hours sleep, thanks to a rousing midnight Quarters tournament with the guys who lived downstairs.

Kevin strolled into the kitchen, wearing a pair of sweat-pants and a grubby T-shirt. His long blond hair was caught back in a messy ponytail that looked as though he'd slept on it, and his face was covered with a few days' worth of razor stubble.

"Morning," Kim greeted him.

He muttered something and opened the fridge, surveying the contents for a long time as though something delicious would suddenly appear.

Then he closed the door again and turned to Kim.

"I need the money for the water bill," he said, lighting a cigarette.

"Water bill?" she echoed. "I didn't even think we got a water bill."

"We do. Your share is twenty-five bucks."

"Even?"

He hesitated. "I think it was, uh, twenty-five bucks and forty cents. I'll check and let you know. Can you pay me tonight?"

"Tonight?" She shook her head. "I'm totally broke, Kevin.

Remember last night, I was telling you and Monica about my bookbag being stolen and how I had to get a job?"

He looked blank. "Huh?"

"Never mind. You guys were totally out of it."

As usual, she added to herself. She'd returned home from work to find the apartment shrouded in a haze of sickly sweet smoke. Kevin, Monica, and Beryl were sitting there chowing their way through a pizza, having fallen victim to a severe case of the munchies.

"Whatever—just pay me as soon as you can," Kevin said, sounding irritated, and wandered into the living room.

Kim shoved her chipped coffee mug aside and reached for her own cigarettes, which she'd left on the table last night. She lit one, inhaled deeply, and wondered what she was going to do for money from now until she got paid, which wouldn't be until Monday.

And even then, despite the fact that she'd agreed to work all weekend—which meant going dancing in Chicago was out—she wouldn't have enough to cover her books *and* the water bill, not to mention buying food and everything else she needed.

Too bad she didn't have a guilt-ridden, wealthy father in the wings, the way Beryl did.

How do you know you don't?

For all she knew, Thomas Kryszka was alive and well and living in nearby Chicago.

And *rich*.

What if she tracked him down and got in touch with him?

What if he wanted to help her, to ease his guilt and make up for all the lost years?

You're sick, Kim told herself in disgust, exhaling a thin stream of smoke through her nostrils.

How could she even consider exploiting a total stranger?

If she ever *did* find her father, money would be the last thing on her mind.

Wouldn't it?

She allowed herself to contemplate, for just a moment, the notion that she might be a long-lost heiress to some fortune.

Well, it could happen, couldn't it?

Thomas Kryszka had been well-off eighteen years ago. How did she know he hadn't become a billionaire since then?

Or even a millionaire?

Or even...

Hell, at this point, twenty-five dollars would help her out a lot.

Not that she was going to find her father and ask him to pay her water bill.

Even if it would serve him right for having ignored her very existence all these years.

If he *had* ignored her.

Again, she had the nagging thought that maybe, just maybe, Suzy really hadn't told Thomas Kryszka she was pregnant.

And if that were the case, it would be wrong *not* to track him down.

For his own sake, not for hers.

Thoughtfully, Kim took another drag and picked up her coffee mug again.

How would she even go about finding him ...

If she wanted to find him?

Which she didn't.

She supposed she could always call directory assistance for the Greater Chicago area, and just ask for him.

For some reason, it was comforting to know that it could be that simple.

Just in case she ever wanted to find her father.

Which you don't, she reminded herself again.

She shoved her chair back, stubbed out her cigarette, and headed to class.

Joe didn't work Friday night, because of his soccer game.

Kim found herself missing his company as she manned the register at Tambourine Man. The other clerk on duty was Vince Frederick's nephew, a self-involved high school boy who spent the entire night talking to his girlfriend on the phone in the back room. Which left Kim to fend for herself.

Not that she minded. The place was pretty dead, and most of the people who did come in only browsed.

When she got home at nine-thirty, the apartment was quiet. Beryl, she knew, had gone to Chicago with several of their friends. Kevin and Monica were out, too.

Kim changed into jeans and a sweatshirt and opened a

beer from a sixpack that belonged to Beryl. She told herself her friend wouldn't mind, even though all four housemates had agreed to buy their own food and beverages and not borrow without asking.

Flopping down on the sagging couch in the living room, Kim turned on the television, something she had rarely done since arriving at Summervale. She turned it off again after discovering that there was absolutely nothing on.

How could they be paying such a fortune for cable—she'd just last week forked over another huge amount to Kevin for that bill—and not have anything to watch?

She sipped her beer, lit a cigarette, and sighed.

It felt good, almost, to be sitting here alone, in silence.

She wondered if she had been partying too hard lately. She couldn't remember the last time she'd gone to bed sober and not woken up with cotton mouth and a headache.

Well, it could be worse, she told herself. *I could be into drugs, like Kevin and Monica.*

She thrummed her fingers on the worn arm of the couch and took another drag on her cigarette.

She heard a faint rustling sound in the wall nearby, and wrinkled her nose. Mice.

Did she really want to stay here alone with scurrying vermin at such close range?

She knew of two parties tonight, but couldn't seem to get motivated to go. For one thing, she had no money, not even the few dollars most fraternities charged at the door for a cup.

For another thing, she'd have to go by herself—not a whole lot of fun if it turned out she didn't know many people once she got there.

Summervale was such an enormous school that there were times when Kim felt lost in the crowd. Sometimes she didn't mind not seeing familiar faces.

Tonight, however, she had a feeling that she would.

She suddenly missed the casual intimacy she used to have with her friends back home.

Friday nights, in high school, had meant football or basketball games, or going to the movies, or dances. There were parties, too—Kim herself had thrown quite a few of the most memorable ones. But those parties had been different.

Back in Weston Bay, she had known everyone in attendance. There had been drinking, but not with as much a sense of purpose as people had at these college parties. Here, the main objective seemed to be to get wasted.

Back in high school it hadn't been quite so . . . deliberate.

At least, it hadn't seemed that way.

And anyway, in high school, Kim had always been able to count on her friends to keep her in line. None of them were heavy drinkers, and they tended to cut her off before she got really wasted.

Here, no one cared whether she was a blathering drunk. Not even Beryl, who, more often than not, was a blathering drunk herself.

Maybe I'll stay in tonight, Kim thought, tapping her ashes into a potted plant on the windowsill.

She could read the new issue of *Rolling Stone* Beryl had left on the kitchen table...

Or write letters to her friends, or call them...

Or—

No.

You need to work on your paper, she reminded herself, as the thought crashed into her mind. She'd forgotten all about it, and it was due on Monday.

If only she hadn't lost her bookbag, with all the research she'd accomplished Wednesday night. Now she'd have to go back to the library and do it all over again. The thought of it made her exhausted.

Tomorrow, she promised herself. *You can go to the library first thing in the—*

No, she couldn't.

She was working at the store tomorrow, from ten until six. And Sunday from eleven to seven.

When was she going to finish writing her paper?

You should head to the library right this minute, Kim ordered herself sternly. *And get up early in the morning tomorrow and Sunday so you can go before work.*

She yawned and kicked off her sneakers.

She just wasn't in the mood. If she went now, she'd be useless. There was no way she could concentrate on boring American history after a full night's work. She'd be fresher in the morning.

She opted for the *Rolling Stone* and for calling her friends.

Then she realized that it wouldn't be easy to reach them.

Allison waitressed on Friday nights, Cameron would undoubtedly be out, and Zara—well, she might be in, studying, but Kim had just talked to her the other day.

She could, however, call Bridget. It was seven o'clock on the West Coast—past dinnertime, but too early to go out. And anyway, for all Kim knew, Bridget was too caught up in missing Grant to go out.

She spent fifteen minutes searching the apartment for the phone number, and resolved for the millionth time to get more organized. She needed to keep better track of her belongings, which seemed scattered throughout the apartment. She could never seem to find anything when she needed it.

That might be a good, constructive project for tonight, since she'd decided against studying. It would get her mind off being alone, which was a strange, unusual feeling.

But she really wasn't in the mood to sort through the mountain of clutter in her room, and anyway, half the stuff was mixed up with Beryl's, so she really needed her housemate to help her. And besides, it would be an all-day project.

You're really getting good at procrastinating, Kim told herself as she dialed Bridget's number.

And that was fine, since she was supposed to be enjoying herself here at college, not engaging in efficiency training.

Just as long as she didn't let herself procrastinate writing the history paper.

But that wasn't going to happen, she promised herself as the phone rang. She'd get up first thing in the morning and get right to the library. No matter what. She'd set her alarm for—

"Hello?"

"Bridget?"

"Kim! How are you? Is everything okay?"

"Everything's great." It was somehow reassuring to hear her friend's sunny voice on the other end of the line. "How's everything with you?"

"Great! I'm so glad you caught me. I just got back from the dining hall, and I was about to go down to the lounge to meet some friends of mine."

"Are you going out?" Kim asked, surprised.

"Yeah, just to this coffee house nearby. My friend Douglas works there."

"Your *friend* Douglas? Is there anything Grant should know?" Kim teased.

"Yeah, right. As if. I'm going nuts without him, Kim. Only a few more months..."

"And he'll be out there for school."

"What I meant was, a few more months and I'll be home for Christmas. But yeah, after that, he'll be coming back out here with me...."

Kim thought she sounded a little dubious. "What, you don't think he's really going to go to Seattle?" she asked Bridget.

"No, I'm sure he'll come, but...I just hope he can get away by January."

"What do you mean?"

"His mother's still a nervous wreck. He's really worried about her. She's been doing all these crazy things, like turning the stove on and forgetting about it, and locking herself out of the house. Grant's worried she's going to get into real trouble without him there."

"Grant's always been way too responsible for everyone else," Kim observed. "Even before this happened. He needs to worry about himself for once."

"Kim, there's no way he's going to leave his mother like this. Would you put yourself first and leave Suzy if she really needed you?"

"I guess not, no." She realized she sounded hesitant, and frowned.

Would she leave her mother in a time of need?

She wanted to think that she was as selfless and caring as Grant was, but she wasn't so sure. And for that, she suddenly disliked herself.

Bridget sighed. "I just hope Grant's mom gets it together soon. I told him she needs to get a job, so she'll have something to occupy herself with every day—"

"Hey, speaking of getting jobs," Kim cut in, "guess who's working as a clerk in a music store?"

"Who?"

"Me!"

"Really? I thought you weren't going to get a job while you're at school."

"So did I, but…" Kim paused, on the verge of telling Bridget about the lost bookbag.

It sounded so irresponsible, though. Bridget would want to know how she could possibly lose something so large and important, and Kim had the feeling she wouldn't think *Because I was wasted* was a satisfactory answer.

So she shifted gears and heard herself saying, "This really cute guy I know offered me the job, and I figured it would be fun working with him."

"Really? Who is he?"

"Just this guy. . . . He's in my history class."

"Have you gone out with him?"

"Not really . . ."

Not really? What are you talking about? You haven't come close to going out with Joe, and you don't even want to!

"Well, what are you waiting for?" Bridget asked.

"I'm just . . . hey, did you hear Cameron's in love?"

Kim realized she was getting really good at changing the subject—not necessarily an admirable skill.

"Yeah, I talked to her the other day," Bridget said. "Tad sounds nice. I told her she should invite him up for Christmas break so we can meet him."

"What did she say?"

"She said she'd wait and see. She didn't seem too confident that he's going to still be around at Christmas. I guess they fight a lot."

"Unlike you and Grant," Kim said. "You guys are ruining everyone's personal relationship expectations by being so blissfully happy."

"We're not *blissful*," Bridget said, laughing.

"Oh, come on, Bridget!"

"Okay, so we're blissful. At least, we would be, if we were

together. And that's not going to happen until December."

"Any chance you can come home for Thanksgiving?"

"No way. I can't afford a plane ticket, and it's way too far to drive."

"Hit your parents up for a loan," Kim advised, knowing that even though money was tight in the Mundy household, Bridget's parents did their best to indulge their kids. All seven of them.

"I can't," Bridget said. "They just found out Elizabeth needs braces, and Cory probably will, too. It's like, I can't even mention the word money to my mom and dad right now without feeling totally guilty."

"I know the feeling."

Kim thought again of her missing father, Thomas Kryszka.

Where was he? *Who* was he? Did he resemble her in any way?

She thought of how Bridget's father and several siblings had red hair and freckles. And how Cameron, whose father was black and whose mother was white, reflected an exotic blend of both their features.

Did she, Kim, have her father's nose and eyes?

She certainly didn't have her mother's. Suzy's nose was sharp—she always joked that it was a triangle in profile—and her eyes were brown, not green like Kim's.

And even though Kim had her mother's fair coloring and slender build, she hadn't inherited her long arms and legs.

What would it be like, she wondered, to lay eyes on the man who had contributed half her genetic makeup? Would she see herself in him?

Suddenly she was filled with an intense longing to find him.
Not even meet him...

Just...

Find him.

See him.

He doesn't even have to see me, she told herself. *I can just find out where he lives, and drive by—or even hang around inconspicuously, and maybe catch sight of him...*

Oh, God, what was with her?

She was pathetic. How could she even consider lurking around some strange man's house, hoping to glimpse him through a window? She'd be lucky if no one arrested her as a peeping Tom.

"Kim?" Bridget was saying.

"Yeah?"

"I asked what you're doing home on a Friday night. It doesn't seem to be a very Kim-like thing to do."

"I know. I was just really tired," she said truthfully, realizing that her entire body was, indeed, exhausted.

All she wanted to do was crawl into bed, pull the covers over her head, and sleep.

And after chatting with Bridget for a few more minutes, that was exactly what she did.

Sunday morning when she arrived at Tambourine Man, Kim discovered that she would be working with Joe all day.

She hadn't seen him since Friday in history class. He looked fresh-scrubbed and upbeat as always, and he was wearing a pale blue chambray button-down shirt and a pair of jeans that looked clean and pressed.

Kim was torn between being attracted to him and being irritated that he looked so put-together while she felt totally thrown-together.

She had on Monica's long, narrow black skirt—which was a little too tight, thanks to her housemate's waif figure—and Beryl's good white blouse, which was a little too big. At least her own black lace-up boots fit, although one of the laces was dangerously frayed in the middle and would probably break before the day was over.

Joe greeted her out in front of the store with a friendly, "Hey, stranger. How've you been?"

"Not great," she said grumpily.

"What's wrong?" He stopped sweeping the sidewalk and looked expectantly at her.

What's wrong is that it's practically dawn on a weekend morning and I've got a raging hangover and the last thing I want to do is paste on a cheerful smile and sell CDs all day.

But all she said was, "I'm just tired."

"Did you go out last night?"

"Yeah."

"Must have had a good time, if you're as wiped out as you look."

"Yeah," she said tersely. "It was fun."

At least it wasn't a total lie. She'd actually been having a decent time at the party before Jake showed up. She'd spent the next hour avoiding him, and the hour after that complaining to Beryl that Jake was avoiding her, and he had some nerve not to even glance her way and acknowledge her presence after what had happened between them the week before.

Whatever *that* was.

Finally, just when she'd decided to go talk to him, she spotted him leaving the party with his arm draped around some drunk and clingy girl.

Kim had done a couple of kamikaze shots immediately after that, just for fun, and to forget about Jake.

The next thing she knew, Beryl was holding her hair back while she threw up in the bushes somewhere between the party and home.

Not fun.

And she hadn't managed to forget about Jake entirely, either. For some reason, she was always fiercely drawn to guys she couldn't have. At least, that was what Beryl insisted.

And maybe it was true.

Take Joe here, for instance. When Kim had thought he was going to ask her out, she'd been turned off. Then he hadn't, and she'd been turned on.

Right now, however, she felt nothing.

Except tired.

And cranky.

"How's the history paper coming along?" Joe asked, going back to his sweeping.

She glowered at him, but he wasn't looking.

"It's fine," she lied again, and stalked into the store to stash her jean jacket in the back room.

The truth was, she hadn't even started working on the paper yet, and it was due tomorrow morning. She'd had every intention of rising early yesterday to get busy on it, but she'd forgotten to set the alarm Friday night. As a result, she woke up fifteen minutes before she was supposed to be at work Saturday morning, and was so worried about being late that she'd raced over to the store without taking a shower.

As a result, she'd felt bleary and stale all day.

Naturally, the last thing she wanted to do was go straight to the library when her shift was over.

Instead, she had gone home, taken a long shower, and relaxed with a glass of wine before the party.

Now, with her stomach still queasy from last night, she regretted not only that wine, but the beer and shots that had followed it. She knew better than to mix like that, but somehow her better judgment had been nowhere in evidence at the party.

That seemed to happen a little too frequently lately.

Well, Kim resolved, she'd keep her head on straight today. And as soon as her shift was over, she'd go right to the library to work on the history paper.

Joe was at the cash register when she went back to the front of the store. He glanced up briefly from setting up the cash drawer. "Would you mind stuffing bags with these flyers?"

She glanced from the towering stack of flyers on the counter to the enormous box full of plastic Tambourine Man bags on the floor beside it.

"All of those flyers?" she asked.

Joe nodded, counting dollar bills.

Kim scowled. Who did he think he was, giving her orders? Vince was the boss, wasn't he? And Vince wasn't here, was he?

"I'll do them later," Kim said, and headed for the section of CDs marked ROCK.

Joe looked up. "Where are you going?"

"I noticed that these CDs were out of order last night," she lied. "I'm going to alphabetize them."

Joe just shrugged.

Apparently he assumed she'd be back to stuff the bags momentarily.

Little did he know that Kim was an expert at making small tasks seem monumental. Back when she worked at the Gap, she could spend an entire evening straightening a sale table, looking busy enough that the manager didn't ask her to clean the bathroom or some other heinous task.

By the time she was finished with the CDs—having ultimately found only two out of order—it was nearly time for her lunch break.

Kind of.

It was past noon, and even though she'd been here for just over an hour, she was more than ready for a cigarette and something to eat.

She approached Joe, who had just finished ringing up a

sale, and waited while he joked around with the departing customer, a young mother with two whiny children in tow.

Kim stood by, thinking that Joe shouldn't flirt with married women. Couldn't he see that this one was ogling him like he was some young gigolo? Did he have to roll up his shirtsleeves so that his tanned, strong forearms were bared? Must he constantly flash that white, easygoing grin?

Finally the woman was gone and Joe turned to Kim with an expectant, "What's up?"

"I'm going over to the Hop to get something for lunch. Do you want anything?"

He didn't answer, and for a moment she thought he hadn't heard her.

But when she opened her mouth to repeat it, he said, looking thoughtful, "Kim, it's not time for your break yet."

She frowned. "What do you mean?"

"You've only been here an hour. You have seven more to go. If you take your break now, how are you going to feel at four o'clock?"

"I'm sure I'll be fine," she told him, thinking that at four o'clock, she'd simply take another break if she needed one.

"You'd better wait awhile," Joe advised her, in a maddeningly mild tone.

"What do you mean?"

"I mean, you only get one break, and if you take it now, you'll be useless later. Especially considering the fact that you look beat as it is."

"Gee, thanks. That's such a sweet compliment."

"I mean 'beat' as in tired, Kim."

"I *am* tired. I need to sit down and get a cup of coffee." *And have a cigarette.*

But she wouldn't say that to Joe. As far as she knew, he wasn't aware that she smoked. And for some reason, she wasn't anxious for him to find out.

Joe seemed about to say something else, but she blurted, "And anyway, since when are you my boss?"

"I'm in charge when Vince isn't here."

"Says who?"

"Says Vince." He wasn't even the type who would smirk his reply—he just said it as if he were relaying basic information, which for some reason irked her even more.

"I spent all day yesterday working with Vince," she informed him coolly, "and he never mentioned that I had to answer to you when he's not here."

"Well, if you want to call him and check, go ahead," Joe said with a shrug. "His home number's taped to the phone out back."

She hesitated, unsure of how to respond to that.

She knew that Joe was probably right. He probably *was* in charge. And for all she knew, Vince *had* mentioned it to her.

She'd tuned him out a lot, having discovered that he was a chatterer.

She hated chatty types, particularly when she just wanted to get lost in her own thoughts, as she had yesterday.

Yesterday, when her long-lost father—no, *sperm donor*—had been constantly on her mind, for some reason.

"Kim . . . ?" Joe prompted.

"Whatever," she said curtly. "If you say you're in charge, then you're in charge. I guess I'll just have to let you boss me around, won't I?"

"I'm not bossing you around."

"Oh, really? Stuff the bags, don't go to lunch," she mimicked him—well, it wasn't really *mimicking*, because he'd been much nicer about it.

But nagging was nagging, she thought stubbornly.

Joe looked at her for a moment.

"So don't stuff the bags if you don't feel like it," he said finally. "Vince will just tell you to do it when he comes in later, anyway. And believe me, if you want to go to lunch, you're more than welcome to go. I think I could use a half hour without your charming company right about now."

He didn't even raise his voice, but it was clear from the expression on his face that he'd had it with her.

Well, that was mutual.

"*Fine!* I'll go to lunch now, then," she flung at him, and headed for the door.

Naturally, her boot lace chose that moment to fray completely through, snapping suddenly and getting caught under her other foot. She tripped and nearly went flying onto the floor, but Joe grabbed her arm and caught her.

"Are you all right?" he asked.

"I'm fine." She jerked her arm out of his grasp and kept going, mortified.

Outside, in the bright October sunshine, she exhaled shakily.

What had gotten into her?

He pushed me, she told herself. *He should have backed off.*

Well, she wasn't going to let it bother her. Joe would get over it.

She had taken a few hobbling steps in the direction of the Hop, doing her best to keep the loose boot on her foot, when it occurred to her that she'd forgotten her jean jacket— which contained her cigarettes, along with the few dollars she'd managed to borrow from Beryl yesterday.

Great.

Now she'd have to go hobbling back in there.

Or you can just keep on going, a cunning little voice said.

She did her best to ignore it, hesitating on the sidewalk and trying to swallow her pride so she could march back in past Joe and grab her jacket.

But the voice became more insistent.

Don't give him the satisfaction of letting him know he flustered you. Just get out of here. Let him wonder what happened to you.

The thought of Joe waiting and waiting for her to come back was so satisfying that Kim instantly started walking.

Across the street.

Down the block.

Around the corner.

As soon as she was safely out of sight of the plate-glass window of Tambourine Man, she bent and tied her broken lace together.

Then she kept walking.

She was halfway home before she allowed herself to stop feeling smug and start feeling...

Panic.

What was she doing?

She couldn't just walk out on a job.

But you hated that job, she told herself. *You hated being up and out so early on weekend mornings.*

And, thanks to the job, she hadn't even managed to work on her history paper, which was due tomorrow.

Anything that interfered with her schoolwork couldn't be a good thing, she reasoned.

And anyway, her mother hadn't wanted her to work while she was in school. She'd wanted her to concentrate on her studies.

Kim kept walking toward home, reassuring herself that she was doing the right thing.

But what about money? a voice kept screaming in her head—a far more irritating and persistent voice than the one that had suggested leaving Tambourine Man behind.

She'd just have to get the money some other way.

She could call her mother. Maybe she had some cash left-over from the evening gown fund....

No! You are not going to bug Suzy for money.

Well, then, maybe she could get another job, something that took up less time and paid more than minimum wage. She could look more carefully this time, and be more choosy. She could even find something that had evening hours, so she wouldn't have to get up so early. Like waitressing.

But what about your bills? the voice demanded. *They're due now. And what about your books?*

She did have over a hundred dollars coming, for the last few days' work at Tambourine Man.

But she wouldn't be able to go back and collect that from Vince.

Or would she?

No, definitely not.

Not after she had walked out on him this way.

Should she change her mind?

No, it wasn't worth going back now, she thought, glancing at her watch. She'd already been gone almost a half hour. By the time she got back, it would be too late to show up as if nothing had happened.

And even if she could come up with an excuse about why she'd been gone so long, Joe would be all annoyed with her. He'd act superior.

No, Kim told herself, *it's too late.*

Apparently, she had quit her job.

And in the process, she'd lost her jacket, ten dollars, and an unopened pack of Salems.

Not to mention three days' pay.

Well, she could stall Kevin about the bills for a while longer.

And she could hold off on replacing her books, too, she realized. She could just catch up with the reading later.

All she had to do was quickly find a new job, one that paid more.

How hard can that be?

After all, she'd landed the position at Tambourine Man in about two seconds.

She'd be able to find something else in no time.

Feeling much better, Kim picked up her pace as she headed home. By the time she got there, she was positively light-hearted, knowing she was free again...

At least for the time being.

Chapter 6

As it turned out, Kim didn't work on the history paper on Sunday afternoon.

Instead, she watched the Chicago Bears game on television over at Gregg and Phil's, reveling in the fact that she was here, with all her friends, eating stuffed pizza and rooting for the team, instead of stuffing bags at Tambourine Man.

And when she got home, and heard three messages on the answering machine from Vince—who was clearly upset with her—she wasn't even rattled.

Not after she convinced herself that he'd get over it, and that she'd done the right thing. She certainly wasn't about to call him back.

Kim didn't work on the history paper on Sunday night, either.

What was the point of that?

There was no way, by then, that she would have been able to research and write an entire paper in time for class on Monday morning.

Which meant the paper was going to be late again.

And if it was going to be late, it had better be good.

It wouldn't be very good if she did a rush job.

So she resolved to spend all day Monday at the library, working on it.

Except...

Except that Kevin asked her again, late Sunday night, for the money for the water bill.

He seemed really angry when she said she didn't have it. Beryl and Monica were both out, so she couldn't hit them up for a loan...even if they did have spare cash, which she doubted.

And she *wasn't* going to call Suzy for money.

No way.

So she'd promised Kevin that she'd see about getting a job as soon as possible.

Which meant Monday.

Which meant that instead of going to her classes, *or* working on the paper at the library, Kim went out in search of newspaper want ads so she could find a job.

Of course, the Sunday paper was what she needed— everyone knew the Sunday classifieds were the only worthwhile classifieds in any paper.

Now, two hours after beginning her search, she had discovered that no newsstand, drugstore, or supermarket in town kept the Sunday papers around on Monday.

Everywhere she went, people acted like she was crazy to be looking for yesterday's *Summervale Tribune*. Some places were actually already out of *today*'s edition.

Kim wondered if it would have been different if she'd started looking early this morning, instead of now, in the middle of the afternoon.

But she'd treated herself to sleeping in, which she definitely deserved after getting up for work both Saturday and Sunday. And it had been well past noon by the time she'd left the apartment.

Now it was almost three. The whole day seemed shot, and she hadn't even found yesterday's classifieds yet.

She'd looked *everywhere*, even the convenience store two doors down from Tambourine Man. Of course, she'd checked to make sure Vince wasn't around before she'd darted in and out of the store, and it hadn't even been worthwhile.

There was nothing to do, she decided, but go home. Her legs were aching from all the walking, and anyway, she was starving. Not that there was food in the apartment.

She was on her way, walking glumly past the small local library branch that was housed in a quaint victorian on Main Street, when inspiration struck.

It occurred to her that the library might have yesterday's newspaper—if not live and in person, then at least on microfiche.

She went in and was gratified to learn from the pleasant, middle-aged male librarian that yes, they did happen to have the actual Sunday *Tribune*. He showed her to the research room, a cozy alcove that must once have been a small parlor. There was a fireplace there, and a weighted mantel clock that ticked pleasantly in the background, boosting Kim's spirits.

She settled into a surprisingly comfortable wingback chair and leafed through the classifieds.

Her improved outlook was short-lived.

It seemed that no one in the Summervale area was looking to hire a hardworking female college student for *anything*...

Except escort work.

There were several ads that said things like,

Date Fabulous Men...For Money!

But Kim knew what *that* meant. She'd read the book *The Mayflower Madam* back in junior high, and was fully aware that escorts were expected to do a lot more than just...date.

She would never stoop to prostitution. Even *she* wasn't that wild—or desperate.

Yet.

Discouraged, she sat back in her chair and wondered what she could do now.

She stared absently across the room, then realized she was looking directly at a Greater Chicago telephone directory.

The words jumped out at her from the spine of a fat book sitting on a shelf in a row of other regional phone books.

And as she gaped at it, Kim realized that she could actually discover, right here and right now, whether or not Thomas Kryszka was living in Chicago.

But do you want to know? she asked herself.

Yes.

She *desperately* wanted to know.

But why? What are you going to do about it?

If she did find a listing for Thomas Kryszka, was she actually going to show up on his doorstep and tell him she was his long-lost daughter?

No way!

At least . . .

Not without first consulting Suzy.

She considered that. What if she called her mother and said she'd located her father—her *non-father*, the sperm donor—and that she wanted to contact him?

She had no doubt that Suzy wouldn't be thrilled.

But *why* wouldn't Suzy be thrilled?

Because she didn't want Kim to get hurt by a man who hadn't bothered to acknowledge her existence for eighteen years?

Or because he didn't *know* about her existence?

Kim contemplated that for a full minute or two, going over every possible scenario in her mind. None seemed very promising.

No matter how she tried, she couldn't imagine her mother giving her blessing and encouraging Kim to contact Thomas Kryszka, regardless of whether she'd lied about having told him.

And her mother had always been there for her, had seen that her every need or desire was fulfilled.

How could she hurt her mother?

She couldn't.

And so, Kim left the library without a backward glance at the telephone directory.

And she resolved to put the matter out of her mind, for good.

Suzy called on Monday evening.

"Am I interrupting something?" she asked.

Just me lying on my bed, staring at the ceiling, Kim thought glumly.

"No," she told her mother. "I wasn't busy."

"Is everything all right?"

Her mother always had a way of knowing when something was wrong. Kim forced an upbeat note into her voice. "Everything's fine. How about with you?"

"I wanted to tell you about the wedding."

"Oh, right! That was Saturday, right? How was it?"

"It was amazing, Kim. They had shrimp cocktail and lobster tail, and after dinner they rolled this little cart around and you could have any liqueur you wanted—I had Kahlua, of course, you know how I love that—and there was an orchestra and everything."

Her mother sounded breathless, positively bubbling over.

Kim tried to muster enthusiasm. "I'm really glad you had a good time, Mom. How was Gary?"

"He was terrific. An excellent dancer, and the kind of guy who opens doors for you, unlike my two ex-husbands. And, let's see, Tony was there—"

"Who's Tony?"

"My boss... Gary's uncle?" her mother said, in a voice that told Kim she should have known.

"Oh, right. Did he have a good time?"

"I'd say. Every time I saw him he was drinking a glass of champagne, and he made the poor bride do the Tango with him. Then he stole the soloist's mike and serenaded her with 'The Way You Look Tonight.' He has an awful voice." Suzy laughed. "Anyway, he was in such a warm, fuzzy mood that I figured it couldn't hurt to ask if I could have a few days off. With pay."

"And...?"

"And he gave them to me!"

"Mom, that's great."

"So I'll be coming to visit you this week, Kim! How does Wednesday sound?"

She swallowed. "Wednesday sounds great."

"Are you sure?"

"I'm positive."

"You don't sound positive."

"Mom, of course I want you to visit. I miss you really bad," Kim said, and that was the truth.

What she couldn't say was that her life was a mess, and she didn't want her mother to find out. Suzy had such high hopes for her—she'd worked so hard to send her to Summervale.

How would she feel if she knew that Kim was throwing it all away?

Tuesday night Kim, Beryl, and Monica were sitting around the kitchen table, eating Häagen-Dazs and trashing men, when there was a buzzing sound.

"That's the doorbell," Kim said. "Downstairs."

Nobody ever used that. Most people they knew came right upstairs to the apartment door, and hardly any of them knocked.

The three of them looked at one another.

"I'll go down and get it," Monica said, and jumped up. "Maybe it's Kevin."

"Yeah, right. He lives here. Like he would stay outside and ring the bell," Beryl commented to Kim.

They both knew Monica was obsessing about the fight she'd had with Kevin earlier; the one that had sent him storming out of the apartment after calling her the nastiest name Kim had ever heard.

"If it is Kevin," Kim said, tossing her ice-cream spoon aside and lighting a cigarette, "she shouldn't let him in. She should just throw his stuff at him and tell him to get out."

"She'd never do that. She loves him."

"We should do it. We don't love him."

"We don't even like him," Beryl agreed.

"You know, that's true." Kim realized Kevin wasn't a nice person. "What does she see in him?"

"Who knows? Especially after he pulled that credit card thing on her last semester," Beryl whispered.

"What credit card thing?"

"Shhh. He used her American Express to order all this stuff online without telling her."

"Stuff for her?"

"Are you kidding? When does he ever buy anything for her, even with *her* money?"

"So what happened when she found out?"

"He denied it. Then he admitted it and said he'd been really wasted at the time and did it as a joke. He said he was planning on returning all the stuff."

"Funny joke. Hà-ha," Kim said flatly. "Did he return it?"

"Nope."

"Who paid off the bill?"

"She wouldn't tell me that. In fact, she'd kill me if she knew I was telling you about it. She swore me to secrecy."

"So that's why she has such bad credit now that she couldn't put a utility in her name."

"Apparently."

"Maybe we really should throw him out," Kim said. "Since we can't stand him and we know he can't be trusted."

"But what about Monica? You know they're going to make up any second," Beryl said, peering into the bottom of the

Häagen-Dazs container, then sticking her finger in. "Do you want any more of this?"

"Isn't it empty?"

"There are a few drips left."

"Knock yourself out," Kim said grandly, then shook her head at Beryl. "If you're that desperate, why don't you go buy another one?"

She knew that Beryl, lucky her, had gotten a check from her father that afternoon. She'd been nice enough to treat Monica and Kim to dinner at Subway, followed by a trip to the convenience store, where they'd bought the ice cream, several candy bars, and a package of Double Stuff Oreos.

The food and junk had helped somewhat to fill the hollow pit that had been building inside Kim over the past few days. . . .

But not entirely.

She was still aware of a desolate sense of emptiness, and she couldn't seem to get past it. The feeling was so oppressive that she hadn't been able to concentrate on anything—not her paper, not job-hunting, not even cleaning the apartment, and it desperately needed it. There were mouse droppings all over the floor in the bedroom closet.

"I can't eat any more," Beryl said. "I'm on a diet."

Kim raised an eyebrow as she licked sticky melted chocolate ooze off her finger.

"This doesn't count," her housemate told her.

"Just like licking the beaters when you're making a cake doesn't count," Kim remembered, thinking back to the high school home ec class they'd shared.

"Now you're catching on."

"Uh, Kim?" Monica stood in the doorway. "There's some-one here to see you."

She exhaled a stream of cigarette smoke. "Who?"

"Me." Joe appeared behind Monica.

Kim's jaw dropped.

For a second—just a split second—she was actually ex-cited to see him. He was wearing a brown leather jacket that made his shoulders look incredibly wide, and a pair of jeans that were snug through the thighs and bagged around the an-kles, just the way Kim liked them.

Then she realized that he wasn't smiling.

In fact, he looked disgusted, having zeroed in on the ciga-rette in her hand.

"What are you doing here?" she asked, forcing herself to sound casual.

"I wanted to bring you this," he said, and she saw that he had her jean jacket.

"Oh...thanks." She draped it over her chair.

"And anyway," Joe continued, "I was worried about you."

"You were? Why?"

Joe cleared his throat and cast a pointed glance at Beryl and Monica, who were hovering, looking interested.

"We should go," Beryl said abruptly to Monica, getting the hint.

"Go where?" Monica was either really out of it, or really nosy—Kim wasn't sure which.

"You know... out," Beryl told her.

The two of them exited before Kim could protest.

Not that she was sure she wanted to. She didn't necessarily want an audience for the scene she was about to have with Joe.

And she *knew* it was going to be a scene. He sure hadn't dropped in for a friendly cup of coffee.

Good thing, because they were out of coffee. They were out of everything.

"Why were you worried about me?" she asked him guardedly.

"Because you vanished without a trace Sunday afternoon. Shouldn't I have been worried?"

"No, you shouldn't have been." She couldn't help feeling a secret little thrill that he'd been *worried*, rather than entirely pissed off.

"You're lucky I didn't call the police," he went on.

"Why would you have done that?"

"You never came back from your break. How did I know you hadn't been abducted by some psycho serial killer?"

"Oh, please. There are no psycho serial killers in Summervale. We don't even lock our door."

"That's really intelligent," Joe said, and she was pleasantly surprised to learn that he could be sarcastic.

"The lock doesn't work," she informed him.

"Even better," he said. "Why don't you have it fixed?"

"We're going to," she lied, thinking that she really should

talk to her housemates about it. Somehow it had slipped her mind.

Joe sighed. "Anyway, Kim, you had no business just walking out of the store the other day. I know you were angry at me, but what you did was really irresponsible."

She had nothing to say to that, knowing he was right.

"Vince was furious," Joe added.

"I'm sure he was."

"He says you're fired."

Duh, Kim thought, wanting to roll her eyes but refraining.

"You'd better tap that ash," Joe said.

She blinked. "What?"

"Your cigarette." He pointed. "You're about to get ashes all over the table."

"Oh."

Like that mattered. The table was sticky and littered with crumbs and dirty dishes.

Still, she tapped her cigarette into the empty ice-cream container, then took another drag and looked Joe in the eye, wanting to appear defiant.

"I didn't know you smoked," he said. "I thought I smelled it on your clothes, but I wasn't sure."

She found herself feeling embarrassed. She hated the fact that he'd discovered something so unpleasant about her.

He thought she *smelled.*

God, how humiliating.

Was that why he hadn't asked her out?

Who cares? an irksome voice protested in her head.

You do, she told the voice. *You don't want Joe to be disgusted by you.*

Why not?

Because who would want someone—anyone—to find them disgusting?

Of course, he hadn't exactly said it in those words, but she knew what he'd meant.

All she wanted was to get rid of him so she wouldn't have to sit here being bombarded by unwanted emotions.

"Look, Joe," she said evenly, "I don't care. I'm through with Vince and the store..."

And you.

The unspoken phrase hovered between them, as pronounced as if she'd said it aloud.

"Why?" he asked. "I thought you needed the job."

"Well, I don't."

"Then I suppose you don't need this, either," he said, waving an envelope at her.

"What's that?"

"Your paycheck. Yesterday was payday. Vince asked me to give it to you."

A cloud of remorse settled over her, and for a moment she couldn't find her voice.

When she did, it sounded small and choked. "He's going to pay me for last week?"

"Why wouldn't he? You worked, didn't you? And Vince is a fair guy."

She nodded, hating herself.

"Here," Joe said, and handed her the check.

"Thanks." She couldn't look at him.

"What about history?" Joe asked.

"What about it?" She stared at her cigarette.

"Aren't you going to come to class anymore?"

"Of course I am."

"When?"

"Tomorrow," she said. "I was busy yesterday morning... studying for an anthropology test."

She glanced up at him when he didn't reply, and saw that he was nodding.

Not nodding as if he believed her...

Nodding as if he wasn't surprised she'd thrown yet another lie in his direction. As if he was totally disappointed in her, but had expected to be.

There was silence.

"Joe," she said after a moment, and then stopped.

"Yeah?"

She hesitated, unsure what she'd been about to say. Whatever it had been, it wasn't a good idea—she was sure about that. She didn't need to go begging his forgiveness, or confessing how screwed up her life had become, or asking for help.

"Thanks for the check," was all she said quietly.

He waited, as though to see if she was going to add anything.

When she didn't, he said, "You're welcome. I guess I'll see you in the morning."

"Yeah, I'll see you," she said.

She didn't watch him leave, just sat there smoking at the table as his footsteps retreated.

When the door closed behind him, she was startled to find that tears were rolling down her cheeks.

Kim's paycheck didn't stretch nearly as far as she'd hoped. In fact, once she'd repaid the money she'd recently borrowed from Beryl and Monica, and given Kevin what she owed on the water bill—and the cable bill, which he said was also due again—she didn't have much left over.

And with her mother coming, she needed to buy some groceries—she couldn't let Suzy think she was starving to death.

Instead of going to history class on Wednesday morning—which would have been awkward, anyway, since she still hadn't finished that paper—she went to the supermarket and bought all her mother's favorites: cream soda and blueberry Pop-Tarts and Nacho Cheese Doritos. She even bought paper towels and a box of tissues—utter luxuries, these days.

She had told herself that once she was finished stocking up on food, she'd head for the library so she could research and write the paper. She knew she wouldn't have time with her mother around for the next few days. And anyway, if she really applied herself, she'd be able to finish writing the whole thing by tonight, before Suzy arrived.

But back at the apartment, as she put the groceries away in the bare kitchen cupboards, she realized that the place was a disaster area. She couldn't let her mother see this mess. Suzy wasn't the best housekeeper in the world, but even she would be horrified by the state of the apartment.

Kim opened the windows to air the place out, cranked the stereo, and started cleaning.

She scrubbed and she polished and she swept, and she even scraped the mouse droppings off the floor.

And somewhere along the way, she started to feel better.

Who knew back-breaking physical labor could be so therapeutic?

She made the whole place sparkle, everything except Kevin and Monica's room, which, as far as she was concerned, was off-limits.

She was in the living room, changing the CD that had just ended, when she heard the apartment door creak open. It wasn't one of her housemates—they would have come right in.

Whoever it was lingered in the hallway just inside the door, not saying a word, almost as though they were listening to see if anyone was home.

Kim felt her heart start to pound.

She knew it wasn't her mother. She wasn't due for a few more hours.

She heard a floorboard creak, and glanced around for a weapon. All she spotted was Monica's heavy Shakespeare anthology, and it was way across the room, on the couch.

Without thinking, Kim called out, "Anyone there?"

There was no reply, and then a floorboard creaked again. She moved toward the hallway, poked her head into the room, and saw Kevin's friend, Random, standing there.

"Hi," she said. "Kevin's not here."

"Where is he?"

"I have no idea."

The guy stared at her, as if he wasn't sure whether to believe her.

Meanwhile, Kim was wondering what he was doing here. He hadn't knocked, and he hadn't called out to see whether anyone was home.

Had he planned to snoop around? Or rob them?

"You can give him a message for me," he said, watching her. "Right?"

She shrugged. "If you want."

"Tell him I don't appreciate being avoided."

She waited for more.

He said nothing.

She raised an eyebrow. "That's the message? You don't appreciate being avoided?"

"That's it."

"I'll tell him."

"Make sure you do." He caught her gaze and held it.

Had she actually thought, the last time he was here, that he had nice eyes?

Now she found his piercing blue stare unnerving, almost... creepy.

"I'll tell him," she said again, hoping he couldn't tell that she was nervous.

He nodded, finally, and left without another word.

Kim wondered what that was all about, then put it out of her mind. She had enough to worry about without concerning herself with whether Kevin was making enemies out of his friends.

Chapter 7

It was wonderful to have Suzy here, Kim thought, staring at her mother across the table. Just seeing her mother again, feeling her arms in a strong embrace, made her troubles fade...at least, for a while.

They were eating spaghetti in Summervale's only Italian restaurant, a semi-dive that nonetheless had atmosphere, thanks to candlelight and red-and-white-checked oilcloth tablecloths.

Her mother had invited Beryl along to dinner, but she was on a starvation diet, having gained another three pounds over the past week.

"Come with us and just have a salad," Suzy had urged. "I'd love to treat you to dinner, since you're giving me your bed for the next four nights."

"No . . . I have no problem sleeping on the couch, Suzy."

"It can't be very comfortable."

"Actually, I used to think it wasn't, but lately, it seems puffier or something. And anyway, I can't go to dinner because I'm literally on a starvation diet," Beryl said. "I'm having only water from now until Saturday."

Suzy was concerned about that, and said as much to Kim now, as they dug into their heaping plates of pasta.

"Don't worry about her, Mom. She's always on some crazy diet. She'll break it. I bet she's home eating potato chips right this second."

"That's not great, Kim. And I don't think you're eating right, either."

"Mom! Did you see how much food I had back at the apartment?"

"Junk food."

She grinned. "That's because you were coming. I bought all your favorite things."

"I guess I don't set a very good example, do I? Eating Pop-Tarts for supper and drinking soda for breakfast most of your life. But then, I've never set a good example for you, Kim, have I?"

Her mother's tone had suddenly gone from light to pensive, and Kim glanced up in surprise.

"What's that supposed to mean?" she asked. Guilt trips weren't Suzy's style, and she'd never seemed to worry much about setting examples.

"I know you smoke," Suzy said with a sigh. "You don't have to hide it, Kim, although it was a nice try earlier, pretending those Salems back in your room belonged to Beryl."

Kim frowned. "How did you know they were mine?"

"For one thing, Beryl has asthma. Don't you remember when she had that attack at our house during your slumber party? And anyway, I've known for two years that you've been smoking. I can smell it on you."

There it was again—someone saying she reeked of cigarette smoke. She scowled. "Yeah, well you're not exactly fresh as a spring morning yourself, Mom."

"I'm trying to quit," Suzy said ruefully, twirling some spaghetti onto her fork.

"You're kidding!" But now that she thought about it, her mother hadn't lit up since she'd arrived a few hours ago. "You quit? Since when?"

"Since Gary told me he thinks smoking is disgusting."

"You shouldn't give up something you really love for some guy's sake, Mom."

"Why not? He's right. And anyway, I may like my cigarettes, but I *really* like him."

Kim fought back a sigh. Her mother was always falling too fast, too hard, for some guy who would eventually disappear. It was totally predictable.

"And then there's the drinking," her mother went on.

"What drinking?"

"Kim, I know you thought I was the coolest Mom on the

block, letting you have a beer at home if you felt like it, and turning a blind eye to those keg parties you used to throw. And I never made any pretenses about being a saint, myself. You knew I liked to go out bar-hopping, and that I had to have my gin and tonic after a long day's work. But I'm starting to think I made a big mistake in raising you."

"What do you mean?"

"My attitude was way too casual. And I'm not naive enough to think you won't drink, especially now that you're here at school, but I don't want you overdoing it when it comes to liquor."

Kim stared at her. "I'm not overdoing it."

"Good," Suzy said. "Because Gary was telling me, the other night, about his college days. He went to Purdue, and he said that drinking plays a big role in the social life at a big school like that. Like Summervale. He said it would be really easy to get caught up in it, and get into trouble."

"What do you mean, trouble?"

"All kinds of things could happen," Suzy said. "An accident. Date rape. Alcohol dependency... I just want you to be a good kid who has her head screwed on straight."

"I am," Kim protested. "I do."

"Good. That's all I'm saying." Suzy sipped her wine, then held her glass up. "See? I probably shouldn't have ordered chardonnay with dinner. I should have had an iced tea, like you."

Yeah? Well, I should have had a beer, Kim thought.

Aloud she said, "Mom, just because you have a glass of wine with your spaghetti doesn't mean I'm going to become some loser. And anyway, you're not an alcoholic or anything...are you?"

Suzy smiled. "No. But I probably could become one. I like to run away from my problems, and drinking's a fun, relatively painless way to do that."

"I wouldn't say painless," Kim muttered, thinking of all the hangovers she'd had lately.

"I wouldn't, either," Suzy amended. "I just wanted you to know that you should basically do as I say, and not as I do. How's that for a Mom cliché?"

"A little late," Kim told her.

Her mother looked up, a distressed expression on her face.

"Mom, relax. I'm just kidding. I'm fine. And even if I wasn't, it wouldn't be your fault."

"Yes, it would. I'm your mother. All those years when I should have been setting a good example, I was smoking like a fiend, drinking like a fish, and running around with a hundred different men."

"So?" Kim shrugged. "You were a lot more interesting than my friends' mothers. Look at Mrs. DiMitri."

Her mother smiled. Kim knew she was fully aware that Allison's mother couldn't stand her, and she knew that Suzy wasn't crazy about Mrs. DiMitri, either.

"And besides," she went on, "you and I got along way better, too. My friends were always fighting with their mothers, and complaining about the rules."

"You didn't have any rules."

"I know. That's the beauty of it." Kim grinned across the table. "Relax, Mom. You did a great job. I turned out just fine, and so did you. We're a lot alike."

"That's because we grew up together," Suzy told her. "I was just a kid when I had you. I was younger than you are right now. Can you imagine the responsibility of a baby at this stage in your life?"

Kim shuddered. "No way."

"I hope you're being careful, Kim. I wouldn't want you to end up pregnant. And I'm sure as heck not ready to have some little kid running around calling me Grandma."

She felt her face growing hot. Despite the open relationship she and Suzy had always shared, she couldn't quite bring herself to get over being uncomfortable discussing sex with her.

"Don't worry, Mom," she said. "I don't even have a boyfriend."

"Yeah, well, you don't need a boyfriend to get pregnant. It can happen just like that, when you least expect it."

"You mean a one-night stand."

"Exactly."

"Was that what you had with my father?" Kim asked. "I mean, I know you said you dated him that summer, but . . . did you really?"

Her mother set down her fork. "What do you mean, did I really?"

"Was he, like, your boyfriend?"

"Not exactly. I mean, we hadn't known each other for very long. But we went out a few times, yes. I told you all about it, Kim. I mean, what—are you wondering if I lied?"

"Well..."

"You think I lied to you?" Suzy raised her voice slightly. "All your life, I've been honest with you, Kim. About everything. I've always told you you could trust me. Why do you suddenly think you can't?"

"I never said that, Mom." Kim was conscious of the couple at the next table looking over at them.

"Oh, you didn't? Isn't that what you're implying by asking me if I really did date your father?"

"No, it's not," Kim said, having lost track of what, exactly, she had been implying. "I just wanted to know more about him."

Her mother stared at her for a moment, then went back to her spaghetti.

"What do you want to know?" Suzy asked after a moment. "Believe me, I've told you everything there was to tell. I wish *I* knew more about him, but he had no interest in me. Or in you," she added, an acerbic note in her voice.

"So he really didn't want me," Kim said. "You told him you were pregnant, and then you sent him pictures of me after I was born, and he didn't reply."

"Nothing."

"Maybe something happened to him."

"Like what?"

"Maybe he was in a terrible accident. Maybe he was killed. Maybe he never got any of your letters, or the pictures."

"He got them," Suzy said flatly. "I called him when you came down with roseola just before your first birthday. I was broke, and so was my father. We didn't have insurance, and I had to take you to a doctor."

"So you called my father?"

She nodded.

"What did he say?"

"Are you kidding? He said no."

"Just like that?" Kim stared at her mother, incredulous. "His own child was sick, needing a doctor, and he refused to help? Why didn't you ever tell me that part?"

"Because I didn't want to hurt you any more than you already hurt," Suzy told her.

"But I never hurt," Kim protested. "I never said I minded not having a father."

"You never said it," Suzy replied, "but I knew. How could I not know? Who wouldn't want a father?"

"I always thought we did pretty well without one," Kim said.

"Yeah, well, I always thought we needed a man around the house," Suzy said. "Unfortunately, my few attempts at finding the perfect daddy failed."

"You mean Alan?" Kim was incredulous. "And John? You married them for my sake?"

"Sort of. I guess I married them for mine, too. No, I take that back. I slept with them for my sake. I married them for yours. I guess I always felt like a failure for striking out the first time, with Tom."

"God," Kim breathed. She had never before considered that her mother was that concerned over the fact that she didn't have a father. Suzy had never let on, through all these years, that it was that big a deal.

Maybe that was why Kim had never thought that it was.

Maybe that was why she had only lately started to realize that something major was missing in her life.

"Mom," she said, "how would you feel if I tried to contact him?"

"Him? You mean Thomas Kryszka?" Suzy fumbled for her purse at the back of her chair, dug into it, then looked frustrated.

Kim realized she needed a cigarette.

"Here," she said, pulling her own pack out of her jacket. She offered it to her mother, along with a lighter.

"Thanks." Suzy stuck a cigarette between her lips and lit it. "I never thought I'd be bumming cigarettes from my daughter."

"It's okay."

"Not really," Suzy said. "And anyway, I quit. Remember?"

Kim shrugged.

Suzy inhaled deeply, closed her eyes, and then exhaled slowly.

"You want to find him?" she said after a long moment and another deep drag off the Salem.

"I'm not sure," Kim told her.

"If you're thinking that he's going to welcome you with open arms—"

"I'm not," Kim said. "I know he didn't want me back then, and I doubt he's changed his mind. If he had, he could have found us, right?"

Suzy nodded. "I've always lived in the same town, had the same last name, listed the number. Just in case."

"But he never called."

"He never called. He never *cared*, Kim. Don't kid yourself."

"I'm not, Mom. I just thought that maybe he should pay for all these years...."

"Revenge?" Her mother gave a bitter laugh, drank some wine. "I've fantasized about that enough times since I had you. I used to think that if I had a gun, and he were standing in front of me, I'd shoot him."

"Because of what he did to you," Kim said.

"Because of what he did to *you*," Suzy said. "I was fine. I got over him. Hell, I never thought he was that great in the first place."

"Well, shooting him isn't the kind of payment I had in mind, anyway," Kim told her. "I just... you know how they're always showing pictures of deadbeat dads on the news? Guys who skip out on their kids and never pay child support?"

Suzy nodded. "But he never owed child support, Kim. Not technically. He never acknowledged that you were his daughter in the first place."

"So? I am, right?"

"You definitely are," Suzy agreed. "He was the only one that summer, no matter what he thinks."

"Well, we could prove I'm his daughter now," Kim said. "You know, through DNA. People do it all the time."

"And that would accomplish ... what?"

"It would accomplish money, Mom. He owes us for all those years when I was growing up. Why should you have had to pay every cent to raise me?"

"I've never minded anything I've given you, Kim. I've worked hard all my life, without complaining, so that you wouldn't miss out on anything."

"I know you have. But it isn't fair."

Alarmed, Kim realized she was on the verge of tears.

And she couldn't cry.

She *wouldn't*.

Not here. Not now. She bit the inside of her lower lip, fighting back the emotion that threatened to clog her throat.

"So it isn't fair," Suzy echoed, reaching out and touching Kim's hand. "Life isn't fair, Kim. It never, ever, is going to be fair."

"But he should pay!"

"Why?"

"Because ..."

"Kim, we did just fine without him. You don't need him now. You don't need his money."

But I do, Kim wanted to protest.

Money would solve all my problems.

Well, most of them.

"I guess you're right," she told her mother slowly. "I don't need his money."

"Then there's no reason to look him up," Suzy said. "Right?"

Kim nodded.

"You know, you'll really like Gary, Kim," Suzy said, shifting in her chair and reaching for her fork again.

Clearly, she considered the subject of Thomas Kryszka officially closed.

"Maybe you can meet him when you come home at Thanksgiving."

"Hmm?" Kim glanced up at her mother.

"I said, maybe you can meet Gary. At Thanksgiving. Maybe the three of us can do something together."

"Maybe."

But Kim's mind wasn't on her mother's latest fling—a man who would undoubtedly break Suzy's heart, sooner or later.

It was on Thomas Kryszka, a man who, no matter what happened, would never break Kim's heart.

Never.

She didn't care about *him*....

Didn't give a damn whether he had ever experienced even a shred of emotion where she was concerned.

She cared about his money.

If he still had any.

And if she ever did look him up, despite her mother's advice not to, that would be the reason.

Money.
Pure and simple.

Kim cried when Suzy drove away on Sunday morning, and the day that loomed ahead felt strangely empty after she left.

The visit with her mother had flown by much too quickly.

The subject of Thomas Kryszka hadn't resurfaced after Wednesday night, and Kim hadn't allowed it to slip into her thoughts.

She had been too busy. She had shown Suzy around the campus, and her mother had taken her to Indianapolis shopping, and to a Notre Dame football game.

It wasn't until Kim walked slowly back into the apartment Sunday that she felt the familiar dark mood creeping back over her.

First, there was the thing about her father—or lack thereof. Now that Suzy was gone, Kim was free to mull the situation over. Knowing her mother hadn't lied—that Thomas Kryszka really hadn't given a damn about her—had left her angry. And resentful. For all she knew, he was living it up in some mansion on Chicago's Gold Coast while she sat here so broke she couldn't even buy the school books she needed.

Then there was the matter of money. Though she had managed to pay her bills and get food into the house, she still needed to replace the books. She would have to get a job, pronto—something that would allow her to work nights and weekends and leave enough time for studying. And fun.

Then there was school itself, which had really managed to fall into the non-priority category lately. She hadn't gone to any of her classes while Suzy was here—not even the ones that required attendance. She'd convinced her mother that she could skip them all just this once, and felt guilty when Suzy told her she deserved a few days off after working so hard.

Meanwhile, the history paper loomed over her like an ominous funnel cloud.

Kim knew she should get to the library right now, write the damn thing, and turn it in first thing tomorrow morning. At least it would be only a week late.

But I have the apartment all to myself for a change, and it would be great to just kick back today.

The Bills were playing Miami at one o'clock, she remembered, and as a huge Buffalo fan, she couldn't just not watch the game, could she?

And then there was her laundry. She *might* have one pair of clean underwear left, and no socks.

Besides, she'd promised Suzy that she'd wash Beryl's sheets and pillowcases, which her mother had stripped off this morning. She knew Beryl didn't have a spare set, and neither did she.

But you can do that later on, she told herself. *And the game isn't as important as the paper.*

And anyway, hadn't she recently vowed to become a more responsible human being?

Yes, she had.

And so far, she hadn't even attempted to get her act to-gether. If anything, she'd let things slide even more over the past few days, using her mother's visit as an excuse.

Well, she no longer had an excuse.

That settled it.

She would spend the day at the library.

She really would.

Just as soon as she'd watched a little of the Bills game.

Just the first half.

The first *quarter*.

You're hopeless! her inner voice berated. *Get moving.*

Okay, she would go to the library now.

Right this second.

She really would.

She searched her room until she found a notebook, some pens, and a highlighter—all Beryl's. Then she scribbled a note to her housemates, saying she'd be at the library all day.

She headed for the apartment door, determined not to be sidetracked this time.

It opened just as she was reaching for it, and Kim stepped back, expecting to find one of her roommates there.

Her jaw dropped when she saw several uniformed police officers.

"Are you a resident of this apartment?" one of them, a six-foot-plus giant, asked.

"Yes."

"Your name?"

"Kim Garfield. I was just going—"

"I'm afraid you're not going anywhere. We have a search warrant."

Chapter 8

"I can't believe it," Monica said for the zillionth time Sunday evening.

Kim handed her another tissue. Monica had gone through almost the entire box in the past hour, ever since Kevin had been led away in handcuffs.

"I can believe it," Beryl said grimly. "No offense, Monica, but Kim and I knew Kevin was up to something."

"We did?" Kim said.

"I did," Beryl amended. "And neither of us liked him. Or trusted him."

"I can't believe it." Monica repeated her refrain, shaking her limp blond hair and lighting a cigarette.

"What can't you believe," Kim asked, "that we didn't like him? Or that he was dealing heroin?"

"Neither. I can't believe he didn't *tell* me he was dealing. I thought our relationship meant something to him. How could he get involved in something this huge and not share it with me?"

Kim and Beryl looked at each other, then at Monica.

"I think the issue here is that your boyfriend was a drug dealer, Monica," Kim said, taking out a Salem. She grabbed Monica's lighter from the table and flicked it, then added, "Not that he didn't *share* it."

"You guys don't understand our relationship."

"What relationship?" Beryl asked, looking exasperated.

"I'm totally in love with him," Monica said mournfully.

"Why?" Kim asked, and inhaled.

"Yeah, Monica, you don't love him. You just—"

"You know what? I don't need to sit here with the two of you, picking our relationship apart!" Monica burst out, standing and pacing across the kitchen.

"Yeah, well we almost got *arrested* because of your beloved boyfriend!" Kim shot back. "I mean, I had no idea Kevin had stuffed the couch cushions with drugs. But the cops didn't believe me."

"No wonder I thought the couch seemed puffier lately," Beryl put in.

"We're all lucky we're not in jail with him," Kim said. "For all those cops knew, we were all in it together. I thought Kevin was going to let them take us down with him—"

"He'd never do that!"

"Oh, yeah?" Beryl asked. "It took him an awfully long time to open his mouth when they were grilling him about us."

"He didn't want to say anything without his lawyer present."

"Monica, stop defending him," Kim said wearily. "He acted like a jackass, and you know it. If he could have sold your soul to the devil to free himself, he would have."

Monica screeched, "He would not!" She stormed out of the room.

"Where are you going?" Beryl called after her.

"I don't know, but I'm not staying here another minute. You guys can find yourself a new roommate."

"*Two* new roommates," Kim said to Beryl after the door had slammed behind Monica.

"Do you think she means it?"

Kim nodded. "What are we going to do? November rent's due next week."

"Maybe the landlord will give us a break."

"Yeah, right. After he finds out Kevin was dealing here."

"That wasn't our fault," Beryl said.

"I don't think he'll care." Kim sighed. "At least this happened after my mother left. I'd feel terrible if she had gotten caught up in the middle of a drug bust."

"She wouldn't have been nearly as freaked out by it as *my* mother would be," Beryl said. "Can you imagine that? I can't even tell her what happened. She'll pull me out of school or something."

"Oh, come on, Beryl. You had nothing to do with it."

"Yeah, well, I had the poor judgment to move in with a drug dealer."

"You didn't know about Kevin."

"I suspected. He's been hanging around with these really seedy characters lately—*way* seedier than Jake and those guys."

"I know, I met this one guy, Random, who gave me the creeps. He gave me a package for Kevin. I figured out what was in it, but I just thought it was for his own recreational use. I was actually an accessory to the crime since I delivered it to Kevin, wasn't I?"

"Don't worry. It's not like you knew what you were getting into." Beryl took a Salem out of Kim's pack. "I'm bumming one of these."

"It's not good for your asthma."

"No kidding." Her friend inhaled deeply. "Neither is coming home and being thrown up against a wall by a burly cop. I couldn't believe it when I walked in and saw them ripping the place apart."

"*You* couldn't believe it. You weren't here when they showed up in the first place. I was on my way to the library— oh, damn." Kim clapped a hand to her forehead.

"What?"

"My history paper. I was going to work on it. I was planning to spend the entire day there, until it was written."

"Well, it's not your fault that you didn't get to. The cops wouldn't let anyone leave for hours. You're lucky you're not in jail."

"I know." There had been a few tense hours when Kim had

really thought she was going to be arrested, along with Kevin. The police kept questioning her, and she kept insisting that she hadn't known anything about the drugs, but she hadn't felt as though they'd believed her.

Then Kevin, Monica, and Beryl had showed up, having just returned from a party on campus. Kevin had tried to run when he saw the cops, but they nabbed him on the stairs. He refused to make eye contact with anyone, not even Monica, and he had been sullen and silent throughout their questioning.

Finally, though, after several hours, the police had worn him down. Not only had he admitted to dealing, but he'd conceded that his housemates had known nothing about it.

"Why don't you just tell your history professor what happened?" Beryl was saying. "She'll have to give you an extension."

"She *already* gave me an extension. It was due last Monday."

"Oh. Not good."

"I know. I can't believe Kevin screwed me up like this."

"I don't mean to lecture you, Kim, but if the paper was due last Monday, it was a little late already, right? It wasn't exactly Kevin's fault."

Kim ignored that reasoning. "What am I going to do? I have to go talk to her."

"Who?"

"Dr. Armstrong. I'll tell her what happened, and maybe she'll take mercy on me."

"Tell her the drug bust was last Monday. Tell her you were mistakenly thrown in jail for a week."

"You're joking, right?"

Beryl shrugged. "I've used more bizarre excuses than that. Believe me, college professors are way more laid back than high school teachers. She's not going to send you to detention or anything, so relax."

"That's true." Kim smiled. "I forgot all about detention. You know, it's pretty cool that there's no punishment program once you get to college. I just realized that no one bugs you about stupid little things like whether you cut class."

"Yeah, as long as you're passing and attendance isn't required, you can pretty much do whatever you want," Beryl agreed. "After all, you're an adult. No one is going to stand over you and make sure you get all your homework done, you know?"

"Suzy was never like that anyway," Kim said.

Maybe if she had been, Kim would have more discipline, though. Maybe she wouldn't be in this much trouble with her history class.

Go ahead, blame it on your mother. Don't take responsibility for your own shortcomings. That's really mature.

"Why are you making that face?" Beryl asked Kim, watching her.

"Because this annoying little voice is trying to tell me that I've totally screwed up."

"Well, don't worry about it." Beryl grinned. "And anyway, just imagine what Kevin's annoying little voice is telling *him* right about now."

They spent the rest of the night rehashing the drug bust, drinking beer, and calling all their friends to spread the news.

Then they realized that Beryl didn't have clean sheets, so they had to find a twenty-four-hour Laundromat and wash them.

But somehow, when Kim finally fell into bed, long after midnight, she remembered to set the alarm.

She was going to go to class tomorrow, and she was going to tell Dr. Armstrong that she simply hadn't had a chance to get the paper done yet, but she had every intention of turning it in by Wednesday.

At the latest.

And this time, she promised herself as she drifted off to sleep, *I really will*.

Avoiding Joe in class Monday morning was surprisingly easy.

He sat down in front of the lecture hall and didn't even glance in Kim's direction.

She found herself staring at him, though—well, at the back of his clean-cut head.

Not that she could help it, since he was parked squarely in front of Dr. Armstrong.

Brownnoser, Kim thought, when he asked the professor to clarify a point she'd made on Friday about "greenbackers"— whatever they were.

She noticed that the pretty redhead seated next to Joe seemed awfully attentive to him, nudging him to show him something in her notes at one point, and glancing up at him repeatedly during the lecture.

Kim found herself resenting her, whoever she was.

Even though she knew she didn't want Joe for herself.

Even though she knew she was tempted to *think* she wanted him, particularly if he was off-limits.

Which he would be if something were going on between him and the redhead.

Was something going on?

He certainly didn't seem annoyed when she whispered something to him as Dr. Armstrong wound down her lecture.

And he didn't seem to be bothered by the fact that the redhead attached herself to him when class was over, following him out of the row and toward the back of the lecture hall.

Kim stood and glanced at the professor, who had been waylaid, as usual, by intellectual hangers-on. She had a minute or two before she had to get down there. If Joe stopped to chat, she'd talk to him.

But Joe didn't stop to chat.

He didn't even appear to notice her standing there at the edge of the aisle, waiting to get out of her row.

The least he could have done, Kim thought, stung, was scan the classroom to see if she'd made it here today. He seemed to have been awfully aware of her presence—rather, her *non*-presence—in the past.

She was so distracted by Joe's lack of interest in her that she almost forgot to speak to Dr. Armstrong.

She turned around halfway to the door and went back, catching the professor just as she was about to slip through the door at the front of the lecture hall.

"Dr. Armstrong?"

"Yes?" The professor turned, looking startled.

Kim suddenly felt as if *she* were the one who'd been caught off guard. She had no idea what she planned to say. She'd intended to spend the class period coming up with something, but instead she'd been busy watching Joe.

Was it her imagination, or was Dr. Armstrong pursing her lips in a way that revealed Kim wasn't one of her favorite students?

But how can that be, Kim thought, *when she doesn't know me?*

"I . . . I'm Kim Garfield," she began.

"I know."

"You do?" Surprised, Kim stared at her.

"Of course I do. We spoke two weeks ago. About your history paper."

"Yes. Yes, we did." Kim attempted an upbeat tone.

"It somehow was lost, and you didn't have a copy. I gave you an extension."

"I know—"

"And the new paper was due last Monday."

"*Last* Monday?"

The words were out of Kim's mouth before she knew where they came from.

Dr. Armstrong gave her a level look and nodded.

"But," Kim licked her lips, "I thought it was due *this* Monday. Today."

She could tell the woman didn't believe her, but it was too late now. She plunged on, hoping to make it more convincing.

"And I was going to tell you that I wouldn't have it in to

you until later this afternoon, because my roommate..."

Dr. Armstrong was still staring at her.

"My roommate," Kim stumbled on, "I mean, yesterday... the, uh, the cops wouldn't let me go to the library."

"Let me get this straight," Dr. Armstrong said, "it's the fault of the *police* department that your paper is late."

"No, I didn't mean that. I mean, it is, but it's, um, it's my roommate's fault, really."

Great. Now you sound like a true genius.

"I see." Dr. Armstrong folded her arms across her stomach. "And that would be because...?"

"Because he was arrested. Yesterday. For dealing drugs. And I swear to God, that's the truth."

Which made it sound like everything else she'd just said was a lie.

Well, it was.

There was a flicker of...something...in Dr. Armstrong's eyes. Pity? Amusement? Anger?

Kim couldn't tell.

All she knew was that she had dug herself in deep, and Dr. Armstrong appeared to have no intention of throwing her a rope.

She shut her mouth, resolving not to incriminate herself further.

The professor just watched her. Silently.

Kim waited for her to say something.

"Dr. Armstrong?" she said after a moment.

"Yes?"

"What...what are you doing?"

"I'm wondering what *you're* doing, Kim. You knew that paper was due last Monday. Not only did you fail to turn it in, but you've failed to show up for class for several sessions in a row. Did you think I wouldn't notice?"

Frankly, she had.

"My mother was here," she said feebly.

"Now it's your *mother's* fault."

"I—"

"Why don't you stop before you've blamed it on the president, or the butler, or *me*."

Kim stopped.

And waited.

In the distance, outside the lecture hall, she could hear chattering voices and footsteps as students headed for their next class.

Why was everyone else so goddamn carefree? Kim wondered. It wasn't fair. Why was *she* the only one in trouble?

And why was Dr. Armstrong just standing around, staring, instead of excusing herself to go off and teach another class or make some other student squirm?

Kim cleared her throat and looked pointedly at her watch. "Don't you, uh, have to be somewhere next period?"

"I have office hours."

"Oh."

More staring.

More squirming.

Finally Dr. Armstrong said, "I can sense that you're troubled, Kim. I don't know you very well—"

You don't know me at all! Kim wanted to scream.

"But I don't think you're a student who doesn't give a damn," the professor continued. "On the contrary, I think you care very much. I don't think you planned to come up to me and lie about why your paper is late. And I think that when you approached me for an extension, you had every intention of complying with my revised deadline."

"I did! Really..."

"Well, then, what happened? And don't start feeding me a bunch of bullshit again."

Kim raised her eyebrows, then found herself suddenly fighting back a tiny smile. Who would have guessed that Dr. Armstrong was human? It was a relief to hear her let go of that formal academic-speak for a moment.

"I just..." Kim shrugged. "My whole life is spinning out of control, basically."

"Personal problems?"

She nodded.

"Drugs?"

"No!" She shook her head. "That was my roommate's deal, not mine. He really was arrested yesterday for dealing. And the cops really wouldn't let me go to the library, and I really was on my way when they showed up. But," she added quickly, "I know I should have had the paper done way before then. It was just... I don't know."

"Boyfriend trouble?"

Kim thought fleetingly of Joe. "I wish," she found herself muttering, and was shocked when the professor flashed a smile.

"Well, is it family problems? Something with your mother? Your father?"

"My father?" Kim shook her head and opened her mouth to respond further.

She was stunned to find that there was a monster lump in her throat, and she couldn't speak.

"Kim?"

"I . ." Her voice broke in a sob.

Oh, dammit.

She couldn't stand here and cry in front of Dr. Armstrong! Or could she?

Somewhere in the back of Kim's mind, she realized that crying might win her the sympathetic reprieve she couldn't seem to score any other way.

And even as she told herself she was despicable to turn her personal trauma into an opportunistic drama, she reasoned that it wasn't as if she'd deliberately plotted this. She hadn't intended to come in here and put on a big emotional display so that Dr. Armstrong would feel sorry for her.

But if it happened, it happened.

After all, she really needed a break here.

She continued to weep softly, even though the moment had passed and she no longer felt a painful stab of loss at the thought of her father.

Hell, she wasn't even *thinking* of her father.

She was thinking that if Dr. Armstrong didn't melt soon, she wouldn't be able to keep up the tears.

What was the professor doing, anyway?

She cast a curious glance up, punctuating the movement with a sniffle, and saw that the woman was just standing there, arms still folded, apparently waiting for her to finish.

God!

What kind of ogre was she?

Kim wiped her eyes on her sleeve and gave one last shuddering sob.

"Are you all right?" Dr. Armstrong asked.

Not like she was concerned.

More like she was...merely curious.

Kim nodded.

"Are you having difficulties with your father?"

"I don't *have* a father."

"I'm sorry."

"Don't be. I'm better off."

"You might very well be," Dr. Armstrong agreed with a nod. "Speaking from experience, I'd have to say that a lousy father can't be much of an improvement over no father at all."

Surprised, Kim looked at her, expecting her to elaborate.

When she didn't, Kim prompted, "You had a lousy father?"

"I had a lousy husband, who was, of course, a lousy father to my kids. Still is. I wasn't able to get out of the situation until a few years ago, when I finally got my doctorate. Fortunately, he's no longer my husband. Unfortunately, he'll always be the father of my kids."

"Does it bother them?"

"Of course. But they're used to it by now. They avoid him, which isn't difficult, considering that he never really wanted anything to do with them, either. Until now."

"Why now?"

"They just discovered a tumor on his kidney. Malignant. It's too far gone for them to operate." She said this without a hint of regret. "Now that he's dying, he wants to mend his fences. But of course, it's too late to make up for years of abuse and neglect."

Kim contemplated that. "I was thinking of finding my father," she said spontaneously. "He didn't want me when he found out my mother was pregnant—they were both teenagers—but I thought that maybe now that he's older, he might be curious about me. Or at least, he could help me out financially."

Dr. Armstrong shrugged. "He might. Or he might not."

"Well, he might not even still be alive, either. Or if he is, I might not be able to find him."

"Maybe not."

Kim was frustrated by her noncommittal attitude. "Well, do you think I should try to find him?"

"Shouldn't you be asking someone closer to you about that? What about your mother?"

"I already asked her. She doesn't want me to find him."

"She probably knows what she's talking about. After all, she knows him. No mother wants to see her children hurt."

"But what if finding my father wouldn't hurt me? What if it would help?"

"Your expectations might be too high, Kim. It most likely won't solve all your problems, and it might create new ones."

"Well, if he could help me financially, it would definitely solve some problems. Then I wouldn't have to get a job. And I'd be able to concentrate more on my schoolwork. If I'd had some financial help I wouldn't have messed up the deadlines for the paper, even."

"Are you sure about that?"

Kim frowned. "Of course I'm sure. I've been really stressed out about money, and I *did* work, for a few days, at this music store, but I couldn't handle that and my schoolwork. It took up too much time."

Dr. Armstrong nodded, but not as if she agreed with what Kim was saying.

No, she looked thoughtful, as though she were deciding Kim's fate.

Which reminded her . . .

"Dr. Armstrong?"

"Yes?"

"Can I please have one more chance to hand in the paper? I swear I'll do it. Whenever you say."

"My inclination is to say no. Two strikes, and you're out."

Kim's heart sank.

"But," Dr. Armstrong went on, "I'm not an unreasonable person. If you want to hand in the paper by Wednesday morning in class, and no later, I'll accept it."

"Thank you!"

"I'm not finished."

"Oh."

"I'm going to have to detract from your grade because of the tardiness."

"What do you mean?"

"I mean that even if it's an A paper, you won't be getting an A on it, Kim. So you had better be prepared to work hard and make it worthwhile."

"I will," she promised.

But she couldn't help feeling disgruntled. It didn't seem fair that an A paper wouldn't get an A just because it was late. Wasn't an A paper an A paper, period?

She'd be lucky if she managed to write a B paper under the best of circumstances, let alone on a forty-eight-hour deadline.

But she had to try.

She left Dr. Armstrong and went directly to the library, determined not to let anything distract her this time.

"Where have you been?" Beryl, curled up on the couch in the living room, looked up as Kim walked in the door just past ten o'clock.

"The library," she said, tossing her bulging notebook onto

the coffee table. She stretched and rolled her head back and forth, trying to release the kinks caused by hours spent hunched over her notes. She ached all over—even her right hand, from clenching the pen.

"What are you watching?" she asked Beryl.

"Monday Night Football. The Cowboys are playing the Forty-Niners. You'll be glad to know Dallas is totally getting whipped."

"Really?" As a die-hard Buffalo fan, Kim couldn't stand the Cowboys, who had beat the Bills in two Super Bowls. She would love to see San Francisco whip Dallas's butt....

"Watch with me," Beryl said.

"I can't," Kim said reluctantly, picking up her notebook again. "I just finished researching my history paper. Armstrong gave me a new deadline. It's due on Wednesday morning."

"How's it coming?"

"I spent the whole day taking notes, making copies, and reading. I'm ready to start writing, and I swear that'll be the easy part, at this point."

"Then watch the game."

"No way. I have to get moving on this now."

"It's so late. Why don't you get up early and do it in the morning like a normal person?"

"Because you know me, Beryl. I'm not a normal person. I'll sleep in and blow it off, and then I'll be in big trouble. She'll never give me a fourth chance. I have to do this."

"Hey, good for you. You sound totally responsible and mature and all that."

"I do?" Kim tried to recall if anyone had ever called her responsible and mature.

Nope.

*Ir*responsible.

*Im*mature.

Those were the usual adjectives people linked with her name.

She grinned.

"Hey, you can use my computer if you want," Beryl offered. "It's way better than your old one."

"I was going to ask you if I could. Thanks." Kim started for their room, then turned back, remembering something. "Hey, have you heard anything from Kevin? Or Monica?"

"Kevin, no. But Monica came and cleaned out her stuff earlier, around dinnertime. She took his stuff, too. I have no idea if he's still in jail or where she's staying, but they're definitely out of here."

"Great. So now we have no housemates and the rent is due any second."

"Exactly. But I won't burden you with that right now. Just go work on your paper." Beryl took a sip from her glass.

"What is that?" Kim asked.

"Gin."

"And tonic?"

"No, straight. I spent my last twenty on a bottle of Tanqueray. Want some?"

Kim did.

Desperately.

She wanted nothing more than to forget about the paper, forget about her money troubles, about Kevin and Monica and the whole sorry mess. She *yearned* to just sit here and get blind drunk drinking gin with Beryl.

But she shook her head. "I can't. I've turned over a new leaf."

"God, you really have, haven't you?"

"Definitely. So don't corrupt me."

Beryl grinned and shook her head. "I promise not to. Here's to the new you," she added, and lifted her glass in a toast.

Back in their bedroom, Kim marched straight to the battered desk between the windows and turned on Beryl's computer. She sat down and got busy immediately, knowing that if she so much as stalled for five more minutes, she wouldn't go back.

And if she didn't get through this tonight—at least most of it—she never would.

So she got busy.

And the writing went smoothly, far more smoothly than she'd expected.

It was actually sort of fun, she decided, stopping after awhile to rub her aching neck muscles and smoke a cigarette.

She'd forgotten that she'd always enjoyed writing term papers back in high school, once she'd resigned herself to doing the work.

Maybe history class wasn't so bad after all, she thought optimistically, after reading over what she'd written so far.

Maybe college could be as effortless as high school, if she could just get back into the mode.

And she was definitely on her way.

As a reward, she decided to allow herself a quick five-minute break, just to go check the score of the game.

In the living room she found Beryl snoozing in front of the television, the empty glass in her hand.

Kim plunked herself down in an uncomfortable easy chair and found that the game was in overtime. Apparently, the Cowboys had rallied, and now they were going to kick a field goal for the win.

Kim found herself getting caught up in the frenzy of the crowd, sitting on the edge of her seat and crossing her fingers as the kicker rushed toward the ball.

"Miss, miss, miss, miss," she chanted as his foot connected with it.

The ball sailed into the air . . .

And then the whole world went black and silent.

Kim gasped.

"Beryl?"

She heard her roommate stir in the darkness. "Hmm? What's going on?"

"I think the power just went out," she said in frustration. "Dallas was just trying to kick a field goal."

"Is it raining out?"

"No. I mean, I don't think so." Kim fumbled her way across the pitch-black room to the window. The street below was dry and the night was still.

"What's going on?"

Kim frowned. "I have no idea." She made her way back to Beryl. "Do we have a flashlight?"

"No..."

"Candles?"

"I don't think so. Where's your lighter? Find it so that we can see enough to look up the phone number of the power company."

"It's in the bedroom." Kim felt her way along the wall and down the hall.

She stepped into the bedroom and realized, with a sudden stab of panic, that the room was dark....

Of course it is, you idiot.

The power is out.

Which meant that the computer was out.

Which meant...

"What was that?" Beryl called from the living room, hearing Kim's anguished scream.

Kim heard her get off the couch and start for the bedroom. "My God, are you all right?"

"My paper!" she shrieked. "It's gone. I'd written half of it, and it's gone."

"Well, didn't you save it?"

"No!"

"No?" Beryl echoed.

Kim shook her head in despair, then heard a thump, and an "Ouch, dammit."

"What happened?" she asked Beryl.

"I just walked into the wall. Where's your lighter, Kim?"

She fumbled for it on the desk, all the while frantically wondering what she was going to do.

How could she have lost everything *now*, when she'd almost made it?

She located the lighter, flicked it, and saw Beryl's bleary-eyed face in the doorway.

"I'll call the power company," Beryl said. "Something must have happened. Maybe there was an accident and someone hit a pole."

"No," Kim said, looking out the window. "Everyone else on the block has power, and the streetlights are on. God, Beryl, is there any chance that your computer saved my paper automatically?"

"Automatically? Nope. Not if you never saved it in the first place."

Kim cursed again, under her breath, and muttered, "I'm dead."

"Just hang in there. We've got to figure out what's going on here." Beryl had found the cordless phone and was dialing by the flickering flame of the lighter. She got the number of the electric company through directory information, then called.

"Tell them to hurry and turn it back on," Kim said.

"Duh," Beryl said. "What, you think I'm going to tell them to take their sweet time?"

"Well, tell them it's an emergency. I have to start rewriting *now*. I don't have any time to waste."

"I will, I will, I—" She paused, then listened, and looked at

Kim. "It's one of those computerized service centers. Press *one* if you have an emergency..."

"It's an emergency."

Beryl pressed one.

They waited.

Then Beryl said, "I'm on hold."

Kim groaned and paced the room, which took some maneuvering since it was a mess and she couldn't see where she was going.

"I can't believe I lost my whole paper," she muttered. It was so horribly ironic that it was almost funny.

Almost.

Just when she'd decided to buckle down and work, the fates had conspired against her.

"Beryl, is this a nightmare, or what?" she asked her roommate.

"Definitely. I hate these computerized things."

"No, I meant about my paper."

"Definitely," Beryl said again, then raised an eyebrow and said into the receiver, "Yes, hello?"

Well, Kim wasn't going to let this throw her, she thought as she half-listened to Beryl explaining the situation to whoever had just picked up her call.

They'd have the power on again in no time, and she'd just spend the rest of the night rewriting. It was so fresh in her mind that she shouldn't have too much trouble getting it back.

"You *what*?" Beryl hollered. "That must be a mistake. We *paid* the bill. Please check again."

"What?" Kim asked in a loud whisper, hurrying over to stand near her friend. "What happened?"

Beryl put the mouthpiece of the receiver against her neck and told Kim, "They said they shut our power off on purpose for nonpayment of the bill. They said they've sent us several warning notices about it."

"They have not! And anyway, we've paid. I gave Kevin—" Kim broke off sharply, and her eyes met Beryl's in the shadowy room.

She knew, then, what had happened.

And so, apparently, did Beryl.

And this time, when the electric company woman confirmed that the bill hadn't been paid and there had been no response to the warning notices, Beryl didn't argue.

Kim sank onto her bed and buried her face in her hands.

How could she have been so stupid? How could she have blindly trusted a loser like Kevin to handle all the utility payments?

Obviously, he had kept the money they'd paid him for the bills. Not just the electricity, but the phone, and the gas, and the water...

If there ever *had* been a water bill, which she doubted.

Beryl hung up and turned to Kim. "They need us to come down there first thing in the morning with partial payment," she told Kim.

"We don't *have* partial payment."

"I know."

"Can you ask your father?"

"No way. I just hit him up for a major amount of money."

"What about your mother?"

"I *would*, except that she's away at some single Republican mothers convention or something. I don't even know where to find her. And anyway, how would she get the money to me by tomorrow morning?"

"I have no idea. I'm waiting for my next Suzy check, but it won't be here for a few days."

"What if you called her and told her what happened...?"

"Yeah, but like you just said, how would we get the money by tomorrow morning?"

"I don't know...maybe it can be wired or something."

Kim shook her head. "Even if it can, I can't bug Suzy for extra money. Not after she drove all the way out here to see me, and anyway, she was broke when she left. She was worried about how she was going to pay for gas on the trip home because her credit cards were all maxed out."

"We're in trouble, Kim. Bad trouble."

"I know."

"What are we going to do?"

Kim was silent for a moment.

Then, giving up her inner struggle, she shrugged and said, "What *can* we do, at least right now?"

"We can drink."

Kim nodded, and they headed grimly for the living room and the bottle of gin.

Beryl poured two glasses, handed one to Kim, and clinked it with hers. "To us," she said.

"And those like us."

"Damn few left," they said in unison.

"Isn't *that* the truth," Kim said hollowly, before swallowing a huge burning gulp of gin.

Chapter 9

When Kim woke on Tuesday, she saw that Beryl was gone.

She rolled onto her side and looked for the digital clock, wondering what time it was.

The clock was gone....

No, it wasn't gone.

It wasn't working....

Because the electricity was out.

Last night came rushing back at Kim. At least, what she remembered of it, before she and Beryl had polished off the bottle of gin. She vaguely remembered that they had toasted all the people they hated, starting with Kevin and ending with...

Thomas Kryszka?

Kim recalled going on and on about him to Beryl, telling

her that it was all his fault that she was in this mess. Had Beryl tried to talk some sense into her?

No, she realized, Beryl had thrown up.

Right in the living room, in one of the potted plants beneath the window. She remembered lying on the couch, the room spinning crazily around her as she cursed Thomas Kryszka and Beryl retched into the plant.

And then they both must have crawled into bed and passed out.

Kim sat up, aware that her head was pounding. It was always pounding these days, but this was worse than usual. It felt as though someone was hurling a sledgehammer at her forehead from the inside.

And her stomach... God, it felt queasy. She realized she hadn't eaten since... when, Sunday? She'd been at the library all day yesterday, never stopping for a meal.

And all for nothing, she thought bitterly, swinging her feet gingerly to the floor and getting up. She stood and swayed for a moment, and her stomach lurched crazily.

I need breakfast, she told herself. *Or...lunch?*

What time was it?

She looked out the window and saw that the day was gray and rainy. For all she could tell, it could be late morning or it could be early evening. And what did it matter, anyway?

She started for the bathroom, calling Beryl's name into the empty apartment.

How had her roommate managed to go to class after last night?

If Beryl could go to class, then Kim could manage to work on her paper.

No way.

"Yes, you can," she told herself.

Tomorrow's deadline wasn't going to go away.

She *could* go talk to Dr. Armstrong. Tell her what had happened. Even show her all the notes she had taken...

But what good would that do?

Dr. Armstrong had made it clear that she was sick of Kim's excuses. She would give her a failing grade, and that was that.

A failing grade...

Suzy would be so...

Not even *angry*.

She would be disappointed, and Kim knew from experience that disappointment from a parent was sometimes much harder to face than anger.

Anger came and went like a summer storm, and when it was past, the air was clear.

Disappointment lingered.

Kim couldn't disappoint her mother. Not after Suzy had sacrificed so much to send her to this school. Not after she had assured her mother, just days ago, that she was keeping up with her classes; that she was studying her little butt off and everything was just rosy.

Her mother had been so pleased.

So *proud*.

And Kim desperately wanted to make Suzy proud.

She raised her chin. She would go straight to the library,

and she would work on the paper there. She'd read some-where that they had computers available for students who didn't own them.

She felt better already.

"I'm sorry," the woman behind the Information desk repeated, "but our computers are limited, and I'm afraid there's a four-day waiting list to use them. That's the rule."

"But this is an emergency," Kim told her, realizing she sounded whiny but unable to control it. "I have a paper due tomorrow morning."

"Well, you should have thought of that earlier, shouldn't you?" The woman raised her eyebrows above her aviator glasses and pursed her bright pink lips. She was one of those smug characters who seemed to revel in quoting *rules.*

"I *did* think of it earlier, and I had it done on my computer at home. But we lost power last night, and the paper was wiped out."

"Didn't you save it?"

"Of course I saved it," she lied, "but that doesn't matter be-cause we still don't have power so I can't use the computer."

"Well, what happened to your power? There was no storm last night."

"I don't know what happened," Kim retorted, "but that's not the point. The point is that the power is out."

"Well, maybe it'll come back on shortly."

"I don't think so."

"Have you called the electric company? They're usually very good about coming right out to—"

"They can't fix it today, okay?" Kim cut in.

The woman blinked. "Well, I'm afraid I can't help you, either," she said curtly, and turned to the girl waiting behind Kim in line. "Next?"

For a moment Kim didn't move.

Fury seethed through her.

Fury at this woman, and at Kevin, and . . .

At her father.

Irrational fury that took hold and filled her with a sudden sense of purpose.

She found her feet carrying her away from the information desk, along a corridor lined with glass display cases filled with alumni memorabilia.

She followed a series of signs until she found herself in the reference room.

The guy seated behind the desk there looked up from the textbook he was studying and said, "Yeah?"

Under normal circumstances Kim would have thought he was cute, with his black roll-neck sweater and longish, wavy dark hair.

But she didn't have time for cute right now, so she got right to the point.

"I need the Greater Chicago phone book," she said tersely. "Do you have it?"

He pointed silently to a shelf, and she saw it there, waiting for her.

She knew she was making a mistake as she walked toward it...

And opened it...

And scanned the pages and pages of "K" names until she found the right one.

There it was...

Kryszka.

The first one was *Kryszka, A,* on South Cottage Grove Avenue.

The next was *Kryszka, A,* in Evanston.

God, who would have thought that there were so many people in Chicago named *Kryszka?*

Granted, it was a big city...

And it did have a big Polish population...

But, still.

Kim scanned the page, past the Adam Kryszkas and the Benjamin Kryszkas, making her way through the unexpectedly *long* list until she reached the *T. Kryszkas.*

She found that there were three Thomas Kryszkas listed; two in Chicago and one in Oak Park.

And then there were the Kryszkas who were listed simply by the first initial *T.*

There were seven of those.

Her hand was shaking as she carefully, quietly, ripped the page out of the phone book, keeping an eye on the guy at the desk to make sure he wasn't watching. She supposed she could have copied the listings onto a piece of paper if she weren't so jittery.

But it wasn't like the page of Kryszka listings was likely to be in demand, right? And anyway, the library would probably be getting a new batch of phone books any day now.

Ten possibilities, she thought as she shoved the folded paper into her pocket and left the reference room.

One of those ten had to be her father.

Her *non*-father, she corrected, and clenched her jaw as she headed home to use the phone . . . provided it was still in service.

"Hello," Kim said nervously, "is Tom there?"

"Who?"

"Tom?"

"You mean Tim? He's at work," the female voice informed her. "Who is this?"

"Actually, I'm sorry, I've got the, uh, wrong number."

And wrong T. Krsyzka again, Kim thought in frustration.

She'd already worked her way through most of the T. Kryszkas, as well as all three Thomas Kryszkas listed. The first one she'd dialed had been answered by an elderly woman who had sounded confused and said that her husband Tom had been dead for years.

The second one, in Oak Park, had been picked up by a machine with a recorded message from a cheerful-sounding teenage girl. Kim had hung up on it.

The third had been answered by a Thomas Kryszka himself. For a moment, Kim lost her voice, staggered by the realization that she might actually be talking to *him*.

But it was the wrong Thomas Kryszka. She found that out when she asked him if he'd ever been to Camp Timberlake.

He'd said, "Camp *what*?"

And so she'd tried again. "Did you meet a sixteen-year-old named Suzy Garfield eighteen years ago?"

"Eighteen years ago I was living in Europe and going through my second divorce," came the disgruntled reply. "Who *is* this?"

"Never mind," Kim had said and hung up.

Now she dialed the last remaining T. Kryszka, crossing her fingers.

An answering machine picked up, and a woman's voice said, "Hi, you've reached Tammy..."

Kim slammed the phone down.

So she hadn't found him after all.

Unless...

Unless he was the Thomas Kryszka in Oak Park, the one with the cheerful teenager talking on his machine.

What had her message said?

Kim dialed it again to check.

"You've reached the Kryszka residence. Tom, Karen, Mike, Billy, and Kristin can't come to the phone right now, but if you leave a message at the beep, we'll call you back later. Bye!"

Kim hung up, her hand shaking.

If Thomas Kryszka—*her* Thomas Kryszka—was still in Chicago, he was living in Oak Park with Karen, Mike, Billy, and Kristin—who was, undoubtedly, the voice on the machine.

Kristin Kryszka.

What a dumb-sounding name, Kim thought darkly.

Almost as dumb-sounding as Kim Kryszka.

If the Oak Park Thomas Kryszka—who lived at 31 Blossom Street—really *was* the right one, then perky Kristin Kryszka was Kim's half sister.

The very idea sent her mind reeling.

The doughnut she'd bought on the way to the library earlier unsettled itself in her stomach, and she sat weakly on the edge of her bed.

How could she have a sister out there somewhere?

She remembered the day her mother had told her that she was going to marry John—John of the three motherless children, the youngest of them a girl.

"Now you'll have a sister, Kim," her mother had said in this fake, warm-fuzzy voice, when she'd broken the news about her engagement. "You've always wanted a sister."

"I've *never* wanted a sister!" Kim had flung at her, because she had been a real brat back then.

A *lying* brat . . .

Since she had secretly always wished for a sister. Or even a brother.

Mike, Billy, and Kristin . . .

"No," she said aloud.

Even if their father *was* her Thomas Kryszka, they weren't her brothers and sister. They were nothing to her . . .

Because *he* was nothing to her.

Nothing but a sperm donor.

The phone rang, startling her.

She snatched it up, irrationally thinking, for a moment, that it might be *him*, calling her back.

But of course it wasn't...

Because she hadn't left a message.

What would she have said?

This is your daughter calling...no, not Kristin...It's me, Kim... the one you didn't want.

The unfamiliar male voice on the phone asked, "Hello, may I please speak to Ms. Kim Garfield?"

And for a moment, even though she knew it was absolutely, totally, crazy and impossible, she actually thought it was Thomas Kryszka.

"This is Kim," she said, her voice sounding tiny and weak.

"Ms. Garfield, I'm calling in reference to your past-due account with the Summervale Gas Company?"

Her mind became a muddled blur.

It wasn't him.

Of *course* it wasn't him.

How could it have been him?

She didn't even want it to be him.

And yet...

"Ms. Garfield? Hello?"

"What? *What* are you calling about?"

"Your gas account is—"

"I don't even have a car, so I don't know—"

"Not gasoline," the voice said, taking on a note of sarcasm.

"The utility. Gas. As in heat? As in, if you don't pay your bill, we're going to have to cut you off."

"What are you talking about?" she asked, though she knew very well.

Kevin.

As the voice went on and on, telling her that she'd neglected to pay her bill and had ignored her past due notices, she bit down on her lower lip to keep from . . .

What?

Arguing?

Cursing?

Crying?

She wasn't sure. She just knew that she was almost to the point that she couldn't take it anymore.

So she simply hung up.

Cut the voice off, right in the middle of some spiel about setting up a payment plan.

Kim stopped biting her lip, and she smiled.

It felt good.

So good that she knew she couldn't sit here and wait for the phone to ring again, or for the water company to show up and shut off the water, or whatever loomed ahead.

She had to get out of here.

Now.

Kim jumped up, grabbed her jean jacket and the few dollars she had to her name, and she ran.

She didn't know where she was going, only that she had to go.

And when she reached the door, she hesitated only a moment before going back...

Just long enough to grab the page she'd ripped out of the Greater Chicago phone book.

The skies had cleared by the time the bus reached Oak Park, a pretty suburb ten miles west of Chicago. As Kim got off and looked around at the other passengers, all of whom walked away with a sense of purpose, she wondered what she was doing here.

You know damn well what you're doing, she told herself. *You're going to find him and confront him, and you're not going to leave until he takes some responsibility for what he did.*

Namely, financial responsibility.

For her.

She thought about Beryl's father. Maybe Beryl couldn't count on him for emotional support, but at least she knew he'd send guilt-inspired expensive gifts and money.

Kim didn't need Thomas Kryszka's emotional support, and she didn't want expensive gifts.

She needed—and wanted—his money.

That was all. With money she could climb out of the black abyss that seemed to have swallowed her.

So what are you going to do? she asked herself as she made her way along a wide street shaded by large old trees and houses. *Are you going to march up to his door, tell him who you are, and demand cash?*

Maybe she would do just that.

She tried to imagine the look on his face, then realized she couldn't even imagine his face.

She wouldn't even know her own father's face.

A lump rose in her throat and she forced it back, picking up her pace and looking around for someone she could ask for directions.

An attractive woman pushing a sturdy blue baby buggy was approaching. She looked like the perfect suburban mother, clad in jeans, a Northwestern sweatshirt, and white Nikes. Her hair was pulled back in a bouncy ponytail, and she was smiling down at her baby.

Kim figured she probably lived in one of the large old homes in the neighborhood, had an equally attractive, doting husband, and more than enough money.

Her mind flashed to Suzy, poor Suzy, who had been an unwed teenage mother. How had she made it through? How had she managed not to demand that Thomas Kryszka own up to his responsibilities, even if he didn't want to be a real father? Why had she chosen to struggle instead?

"Excuse me," Kim called as the woman and buggy approached. "Can you tell me where Blossom Street is?"

She stopped. "Sure. It's, let me see . . . about a mile down that road"—she pointed at an intersection—"and then you go into the first development you come to on the right, and Blossom is one of the streets in there."

"Thanks." A mile down the road? Kim hadn't realized Oak

Park was that big. She'd really have to go out of her way to find him.

As if you haven't gone out of your way already, an inner voice retorted. *You've been on three buses in the past four hours just to get here.*

And now that she had come this far...

"Do you go to Summervale?" the woman asked, and Kim looked up at her, startled.

"How did you know that?"

"Your shirt," she said, pointing at the sweatshirt Kim had borrowed from Beryl's closet. "My husband's brother is a senior there."

"Really?"

She nodded. "He loves it. What year are you in?"

"Freshman."

"Do you like it?"

"So far," Kim said, finding it surprising that she could possibly be standing here making small talk with a stranger in the midst of her emotional turmoil.

"I loved college," the woman said. "I went to Northwestern. So did Jim—my husband. That's where we met—at freshman orientation."

"That's nice." Kim wondered what it would be like to meet the man you were going to marry when you were so young. It would be like her marrying Jake—or Joe.

Hardly likely, since they both hated her.

"Well, thank you for the directions," she said restlessly.

"No problem."

A tiny cry erupted from the baby carriage, and the woman immediately bent over.

Kim found herself peering over the edge of the buggy, catching a glimpse of a small bundle wrapped in pink. "How old is she?" she asked the woman as the baby squeezed her eyes closed and opened her mouth in a gigantic yawn.

"Two months. Isn't she the most precious thing?"

Kim smiled. "She's really cute."

"She's our little cuddle-cat, aren't you? Aren't you?" She looked up at Kim a little sheepishly. "That's what Jim calls her."

"That's sweet."

There was that lump again, rising unexpectedly in Kim's throat and forcing her to make a quick getaway from the perfect mom with her perfect baby and perfect life.

Cuddle-cat.

When she was about twelve, that little girl was going to hate having her father call her that. She'd turn red and she'd mutter, "Dad, stop it!" and when he tried to hug her, she'd wriggle away to go join her friends.

Kim had seen that happen countless times with her friends back home, who were all embarrassed by their fathers at one point or another. Especially Allison, whose father had once shown up at a party when she'd missed her curfew.

Growing up, Kim had always been kind of glad that she didn't have to deal with that.

Now she felt a pang in the vicinity of her heart, followed by a flood of envy for tiny pink Cuddle-cat.

I hope you know how lucky you are, she silently told the baby, turning to look over her shoulder. She watched the retreating mother and child until they turned a corner and vanished from sight.

The house at 31 Blossom Street was a two-story colonial that was identical to the houses next door and across the street, except for the color. It was painted a pale blue, with white trim and a white front door.

There was a small front lawn shaded by two maple trees, bisected by a curving brick path leading up to the small porch. The lawn was dotted with a few leaves, and there was a big pile by the curb, as though someone had recently raked. A bike was parked in the empty driveway, and there was a basketball hoop over the attached garage, and a wooden deck was visible behind the house.

To the right of the door was a white plaque. Even standing on the sidewalk by the street, Kim could read it.

Welcome.

It was such a corny, impersonal sign.

Welcome.

She was sure that whoever had hung it there hadn't meant it to include a long-lost illegitimate daughter.

Kim realized she was standing and staring, so she started walking again, past the house, down the block, past the other cookie-cutter houses in the development. Some were white and some were yellow and one was pale pink.

But the Kryszka home was the only blue one on the street, and when she turned back at the end of the street she could see it easily.

It might not even be his house, she reminded herself. *It might be some other Thomas Kryszka.*

But somehow, deep inside, she knew it was where *he* lived.

Here, in comfortable, upper-middle class suburbia, with his wife and his three children.

A real family; a normal family. Two parents, and siblings.

Nearby, she could hear children playing on a backyard swingset, and a car door slamming, and birds chirping.

Comfortable, homey sounds.

Kim swallowed. Hard.

She fumbled in her pocket for her pack of Salems, lit one, and inhaled deeply.

And she looked at the blue house.

She noticed that the paint job was recent, and thought of how badly the paint was peeling at Suzy's house back in Weston Bay.

March right back there, she ordered herself, staring at the pretty blue house with the white shutters. *Ring the doorbell and tell them who you are.*

But he probably wasn't even home, she argued mentally. It was late afternoon. He must be at work.

Maybe no one was home.

If that was the case, then she could march back there and ring the bell, and when no one answered, she could leave.

She would know that she had come here, and she had tried.

Tried what?

Tried to claim what belongs to you, she told herself firmly. *A piece of this life.*

No!

You don't want to be part of this life. Not part of his life. And you don't want him to be a part of yours.

She just wanted him to help her.

She just knew that if he would help her, everything would be all right.

All she needed was his money.

And what do you expect? she asked herself. *That he's going to answer the door, listen to your little speech, write you a check, and say, "Okay, nice meeting you, bye"?*

It *could* happen.

He might want to give her the money to get rid of her fast, so that she wouldn't complicate his nice, perfect suburban life.

Did his wife even know he had a daughter out there somewhere? Did his kids know they had a half-sister?

Probably.

No . . .

Probably not.

He wouldn't be the type who'd want to deal with such unnecessary complications. He would have simply kept Kim's existence to himself. . . .

If he even remembered her.

She took a drag on her cigarette.

How could a person forget that they had a child?

It seemed impossible...

And yet...

How could a person *not care* that they had a child?

That seemed even more impossible, but it was what Thomas Kryszka had done.

Kim started walking again, slowly, toward the house.

He owes you, a voice said forcefully in her head. *You need to make him pay.*

But...how much?

Two hundred dollars would allow her to pay her share of the bills and to replace her books....

But there would be more bills.

And next semester, more books.

And then there were all the things he should have been there to provide.

What price tag should she put on all the years he hadn't been there to give her birthday and Christmas presents, and clothes and shoes and toys, and vacations, and piano lessons, and the braces the orthodontist had said she needed, but that Suzy couldn't afford?

You did all right without the braces, she pointed out. Her teeth *were* slightly crowded, but you couldn't tell by looking at her, and she'd never had a problem chewing or speaking.

In fact, back when she was in junior high, she'd been *glad* her mother couldn't afford the braces. Who wanted a mouthful of metal, anyway?

She was drawing closer to the house, staring at it. She

could see the sign by the front door again. She couldn't read it from this distance, but she knew what it said.

Welcome.

Yeah, right.

Kim stopped on the sidewalk directly in front of the house again.

Go ahead. Go ring the doorbell, or knock, or whatever it is that you want to do.

No, I don't want to do it, she argued with herself. *I have to.*

Why?

Because he owes me.

And I'm in trouble.

And I can't get out without his help.

She frowned.

Was that the truth?

Was Thomas Kryszka, Sperm Donor and Disappearing Dad, really the only answer to her problems?

Kim's eyes narrowed and she brought her fist up to her mouth, pressing it against her lips as she stared at the house.

He has money, she told herself. *I don't.*

And money is the answer to my problems.

Right?

Right?

She felt tears forming in the corners of her eyes.

With money, she could pay off the bills and buy her books.

But then, there was still the paper that was due tomorrow morning.

And there were still the classes she couldn't seem to attend, and the partying she couldn't seem to avoid.

And there was Joe, who was no longer interested in her, if he ever had been.

Money wouldn't change any of those things.

So this is it, then? she wondered in despair. *I'm just stuck with my lousy life the way it is? There's nothing I can do to make it better?*

How could that be?

She was crying now, really crying; her shoulders heaving and her body quaking with the giant sobs that rolled over her relentlessly.

She tossed her cigarette to the sidewalk and ground it out with her heel, then hugged herself, wrapping her arms up around her shoulders as if she could stop the trembling.

She didn't know how long she stood that way, or whether anyone saw her.

She didn't even care.

She only knew that when it was over, when the crying stopped, she knew what she had to do.

The answer was clear in her mind; so clear she couldn't believe it had taken her this long to realize that what she needed wasn't Thomas Kryszka's money.

It was his love.

She needed a father, a daddy, someone who would call her Cuddle-cat and ruffle her hair and embarrass her in front of her friends.

But Thomas Kryszka couldn't give her that.

He might be willing to give her money, but he could never give her love.

Even if he wanted to; even if enough time had passed for him to realize he'd made a mistake....

It was too late.

He'd missed his chance.

He could never be Kim's dad.

Kim would never have a dad.

Nothing she could do, nothing *he* could do—even if he wanted to—was going to change that.

Kim glanced up at the blue house again.

She sniffled, then wiped her nose on the sleeve of Beryl's sweatshirt.

Then she turned and walked away.

Chapter 10

"Dr. Armstrong?"

"Yes?"

The instructor, on her way to her office, turned around and saw Kim. Her eyes widened, then narrowed.

"I wanted to give you this." Kim handed her the paper-clipped stack of notebook paper, filled with line after line of her handwriting, in pen and then in the pencil she'd changed to when the ink had run out.

"What is it?" Dr. Armstrong asked, frowning.

"It's my paper." She cleared her throat. "I just finished it... which is why I wasn't in class this morning. I've been up all night, working on it."

The professor was silent, glancing over the first page.

Kim noticed that she was wearing a crisply ironed ivory

linen blouse and tailored navy pants with a matching blazer. Her hair was brushed smoothly back into a clip, and her earrings coordinated with the bracelet on her left wrist and the watch on her right. She smelled faintly of mint and of honeysuckle perfume.

Kim felt more stale and rumpled than ever, standing beside her, waiting for her to comment. All she wanted to do was go back to the apartment, take a hot shower, climb into bed, and sleep until next week.

"I had asked that the papers be typed," Dr. Armstrong commented, flipping to the next page, and then the next.

"I know . . . I tried."

Kim opened her mouth again to tell Dr. Armstrong just what had happened; exactly how hard she had tried to use a computer or typewriter; and how the fates had obviously been conspiring against her.

Then she clamped her mouth shut. Dr. Armstrong wasn't interested in excuses, even if they were real.

"I'm going to have to lower your mark a half grade for not typing," the teacher said.

Kim wanted to protest that it wasn't fair of her to do that. But she didn't.

"And then there's the markdown for turning it in late," Dr. Armstrong said. "I can't do anything about that, Kim. I can't bend my rules for you, or for anyone else."

Kim nodded.

"I only hope," the woman went on, "that this paper is worth my time and yours."

"It will be," Kim said firmly, though she wasn't so sure.

How wonderful could it be, when she had started it late last night after the four-hour bus trip home from Oak Park? And she'd written it sitting in the Hop, which was open twenty-four hours, knowing the power would still be out back at home.

She'd drunk cup after cup of coffee, and smoked a pack and a half of cigarettes as she worked nonstop through the wee hours of the morning and well past dawn.

She'd finally finished writing just an hour ago, too late to make it to history class. But she'd remembered that Dr. Armstrong had office hours immediately after, and she'd rushed over to campus to intercept her here.

"Out of curiosity," Dr. Armstrong said, "why did you put off writing the paper until last night, Kim?"

"I didn't. I've been trying to work on it, but things keep going wrong." Her voice broke and she fought back tears, knowing they wouldn't make a difference.

Not out here in the real world, where nobody ever cut you a break.

"Things are always going to go wrong," Dr. Armstrong said in a matter-of-fact way. "The best we can do is be prepared for the worst."

It sounded like some old-fashioned quote someone's grandmother would use, Kim thought.

"That means thinking ahead, Kim," Dr. Armstrong went on. "It means keeping up with our responsibilities. No matter what."

"I know." Kim studied her feet, clad in the sneakers that had carried her all over Oak Park yesterday. They were scuffed and muddy, and her feet ached.

"What have you decided to do about your father?"

The sudden question caught her off guard, and she looked up at Dr. Armstrong. "What?"

"Your father. You said the other day that you were considering looking for him."

"Oh. I was, but . . . I decided not to."

"Why is that?"

"Because . . ." She shrugged. How could she put it into words? Especially for this woman, who was, after all, a virtual stranger?

Dr. Armstrong was waiting.

"I figured out that I don't need him after all," Kim told her.

The woman tilted her head, studying Kim, then said, "I'm sure that's a wise decision." She tucked Kim's paper into the brown leather satchel over her shoulder. "I look forward to reading your paper, Kim."

She nodded. "I hope it's okay."

"So do I. And I'll see you in class on Friday. Don't forget about the test."

What test?

Kim almost asked aloud, but caught herself in time. She just nodded again. "I won't forget."

"Good. Have a nice day." Dr. Armstrong turned and walked briskly away.

Kim sighed heavily and headed in the opposite direction.

She had expected to feel lighthearted after finishing and turning in the paper. After all, she'd worked her butt off, and she'd accomplished what she'd set out to do.

Why wasn't she exhilarated?

I'm just tired, she told herself.

Beryl was in the apartment when Kim got there, standing in front of the open refrigerator door.

"Where have you been?" she asked, looking up as Kim walked into the kitchen.

"Long story. What's that smell?"

"Disgusting spoiled food, from the fridge being warm for two days. I'm throwing away every single thing in here."

"I didn't even know we *had* anything in there."

"Neither did I. Pretty ironic, isn't it? You don't know you have food until it's gone bad."

Kim nodded and thought there was a lesson in there somewhere, but she was too numb to figure out what it was.

"You didn't tell me where you've been." Beryl tossed a small jar of something into the garbage.

Kim paused, then said simply, "Working on my paper."

"All night? Where? At the library?"

Kim hesitated, then nodded. She was suddenly too exhausted to speak, and even if she weren't, she didn't want to share what had happened in Oak Park.

Not with Beryl.

Maybe not with anyone.

"So did you hand it in?"

"What?"

"What else? The paper."

"Yes. And now I'm going to take a shower and go to bed."

"Good idea. You seem really out of it. But, hey, wait, before you go you should know..."

Kim stopped in the doorway. "What?"

"I got the money for the electric bill, and for the gas bill—they called yesterday, looking for you, by the way. They said you'd hung up on them."

"I did."

"Really? How come?"

"I just couldn't deal with it," Kim said with a shrug.

Beryl looked vaguely irritated. "Well, I smoothed things over, and they said they'll arrange a payment plan, and they won't turn off the gas."

"Good. Thanks."

"And the electricity should be back on shortly, since I paid the bill this morning."

"How'd you get the money?"

"I gave in and called my father and got him to wire it to me. He had just bought himself a plasma television. I made him feel really guilty." Beryl shrugged. "He's such a loser."

"I'll pay you my share of it as soon as I can," Kim said.

Beryl nodded, and again that vaguely annoyed expression darted across her face. "Look, Kim, go get some sleep. When you wake up we can figure out what we're going to do about the housemate fiasco."

"Oh, yeah...I forgot all about that." Kim was too tired to let her mind zero in on any more problems.

She stood under the hot shower for a long time, thinking that she had to be sure to wake up in time for her afternoon English comp class. From now on, she was going to attend every single lecture on her schedule, every single day. No matter what.

She thought about setting the alarm, just to make sure she didn't sleep through, then realized she couldn't, because the power still wasn't on.

She could go into the kitchen and ask Beryl to wake her....

But she just couldn't seem to walk another step.

And anyway, she'd definitely wake up in time for class. That was hours away.

She sank into bed, pulled the quilt up around her head, and fell asleep.

She dreamed that she was a little girl again, and that some-one big and strong was rocking her in his arms, stroking her hair and calling her Cuddle-cat.

The room was shadowy when Kim woke. It must be dusk, she realized. She had missed her English class.

She sat up and stretched.

Then she saw Beryl curled up, asleep, in the bed across from hers.

She was taking a nap? She rarely did that.

Kim got out of bed and walked over to the window, looking out at the street.

It was oddly deserted for early evening, she thought.

Unless...

Maybe it *wasn't* early evening after all.

Maybe it was early morning.

Maybe Beryl wasn't taking a nap; maybe she was just... sleeping.

Could Kim have actually slept through an entire day and night? She *did* feel rested, if not entirely refreshed. She couldn't remember the last time she'd felt refreshed.

She found Beryl's watch on the dresser and peered at it in the dim light from the window.

Five-thirty.

And she could see a sliver of pinkish-orange sun off toward the right....

Which told her nothing, because she didn't know whether she was looking east or west. She'd never paid attention.

And at this time of year, right before the autumn equinox, the sun rose and set at roughly the same time.

Right around five-thirty.

For a moment, Kim just stood there in the middle of the bedroom, confused.

Then she was struck by the absurdity of the situation.

She didn't know if the sun was coming up or going down.

She didn't know if it was day or night.

How could she not be aware of something so basic?

How could her life be *that* screwed up?

It was almost laughable, she thought as she went into the bathroom and brushed her teeth, something that felt necessary whether it was morning or evening.

When she came out after washing her face and brushing her hair, she saw that the light slipping in the bedroom window was definitely brighter.

So it *was* morning.

Okay.

She had to go to anthropology class, but not until...

Ten?

Eleven?

It had been so long since she'd gone that she couldn't remember. And her schedule had been in her bookbag....

Which meant that it was gone for good.

What was she supposed to do now? She couldn't even remember exactly which lecture hall anthropology was in, and she didn't know a soul in the class.

She would just have to go over to the science building and try to figure things out, she decided.

But not for a few more hours.

Which meant she had a lot of time to kill.

She decided she should use it wisely.

Which meant...

What?

She couldn't study, because she didn't have her books, or any notes.

She couldn't clean her room, because Beryl was still sleeping in there.

She couldn't even call one of her friends, because everyone she knew would be in bed at this hour.

Her stomach growled.

She realized she was starving. The last thing she'd swallowed had been her final cup of coffee at the Hop yesterday morning.

What she wouldn't do for a plate of eggs and hash browns right now. That was what the waitress had been serving to a man in the next booth when Kim was finally packing up her notes yesterday.

There was no reason she couldn't go down to the restaurant right now and have breakfast, was there?

She mulled over that idea. She had a few dollars left, and she *was* hungry.

And it would be kind of fun to go out to eat, alone, at this hour.

Kind of a celebration of her turning over a new leaf.

Her mind made up, Kim headed for the bedroom to get dressed.

The coffee shop was crowded with senior citizens and early-bird joggers and bleary-eyed night workers just coming off their shifts. The booths were full, so Kim slid onto a stool at the counter.

"Be with you shortly, hon," said the waitress, tossing a menu in front of her.

Kim nodded and didn't bother to look at it. She knew just what she wanted. The eggs and hash browns, with white toast, grape jelly, and a side of ham.

And orange juice.

And coffee.

She lit a cigarette and looked around at the bustling place. It seemed sort of cheerful, all these people coming together so early in the day. Kim hadn't noticed any of the details yesterday; she'd been too wrapped up in writing her paper.

But today, she saw the grandfatherly regulars who came in alone with newspapers under their arms, sat at the counter, and greeted the waitresses like old friends. She smelled the comforting aroma of frying bacon and perking coffee, and she heard the clattering plates and the chattering people in the booths.

"Sorry, I'm getting to you, hon," the waitress called to Kim as she passed by.

Kim nodded again and took a drag on her cigarette, which didn't taste great at this hour of the day, on an empty stomach. She stubbed it out and busied her hands straightening the sugar packets in a container on the counter. Then she worked on the compartments of jelly, organizing them by flavor.

"Hey, you're pretty good at that," the waitress said, finally showing up with a pot of coffee and her order pad. She was a pleasant-looking middle-aged woman with bright blue eyes. "You want a job?"

Kim blinked. "A job? Here?"

"I was just kidding," the waitress said, tossing her blond ponytail and smiling, "unless you're interested? Because we actually do need someone."

"To wait tables?"

"Yup. A girl quit the other day, which is why we're short-handed, which is why I'm finally here to say, what do you want?"

Kim told her the order, then asked, "What are the hours?"

"Hmm? Oh, you mean the job? You really looking for work?"

"Desperately."

"The hours would be the same as mine, hon. The early bird breakfast shift. Four-thirty to nine."

"Oh . . . forget it."

"Yeah? Why?"

"I could never get up that early every day."

"It's only weekdays. And the tips are great because we're always busy. And anyway, you're up now, aren't you?"

"I guess, but this is a fluke," Kim told her. "And anyway, I have classes in the mornings."

"What time?"

Kim thought about that. "Not until ten, but—"

"You'd be off at nine," the woman told her again. "Give it some thought. We're pretty short-handed, and I know he wants to hire someone right away. And once you get used to it, it's not so bad to get up early."

"I'm sure it's not," Kim said, thinking she had no intention of finding out.

"Well, if you decide you want the job, come back and ask for Fritz. He's the manager."

"Yeah, sure."

"Decaf, or regular?" the waitress asked, flipping over the coffee mug that sat in a saucer in front of Kim.

"Regular. Definitely."

It was going to be a long day.

Anthropology, as it turned out, was at eleven o'clock in Room 103.

Kim, who had slipped into a ten o'clock lecture in Room 102, convinced she was in the right place at the right time, hadn't realized it was the wrong place, wrong time, until it was too late to get up and walk out.

She wasn't thrilled to have sat through an advanced lesson in Physics.

The professor hadn't even noticed she was there, but a few of the students had given her odd looks.

Now that she was finally in the right classroom, she decided things were looking up...

Until she found out about the test.

The one she hadn't realized was scheduled for today.

She stared at the first question, a multiple choice about ancient astronaut evidence on the Nazca Plains. She hadn't the faintest idea whether the answer was A, B, or C.

But with multiple choice, she at least had a thirty-three percent chance of making a correct guess.

She'd be fine, as long as the whole test was multiple choice, she thought, flipping to the second page.

There, she found SECTION II—fill in the blanks.

Followed by SECTION III—essays.

She was going to fail the test.

Somehow, she managed to get through the hour, completing her test to the best of her ability . . .

Which wasn't saying much, since she hadn't kept up with the reading and had never heard of half the topics that were covered.

After class she was heading dismally across the Quad when she heard a familiar voice say, "Hey, Kim, how's it going?"

She looked up and saw Joe. He had a bookbag over his shoulder, and he was wearing that brown leather jacket again, the one that made his shoulders look so broad.

"It's going fine," she lied. "How about you?"

"Okay. Where are you coming from?"

"Intro to anthropology."

"Hey, I took that last year. Great class, huh?"

"Yeah, great," she said hollowly. "So what's going on?"

"We have a soccer game this afternoon. You coming?"

She brightened. Was he interested in her after all?

"I hadn't planned on it," she said.

"You should."

"Maybe I will," she told him, then tried to think of something else to say. "How's work going?"

Oh, great. Why had she brought *that* up? The last thing she wanted to discuss was Tambourine Man.

"It's going fine," he said. "Busy."

"Oh, yeah?"

"Did you find another job?"

"Me? No."

"They're looking for a waitress at the Hop."

"What are you, a walking classified section?" she asked, remembering the day he'd told her about the job at Tambourine Man.

He didn't smile at that. "I work right next door," he said simply. "One of the waitresses told me they're short-handed."

"Well, I can't be a waitress at the Hop," Kim told him.

"Why not?"

"Too much fifties stuff. I'd overdose on all that shoo-bop music."

"It's not so bad—"

"And anyway, it's the early shift."

"You have someplace else to be at that hour of the morning?"

"Yeah. Bed," she retorted, and grinned.

Joe didn't grin back. "Well, I thought if you really needed a job . . ."

"What makes you think I'm that hard up?"

"I don't know . . . I just got the impression that you were looking for money."

"Who isn't?" She tried to sound flip, but it wasn't coming out that way. "You know, I have to run. I have to get to basic algebra."

"Wow, two classes in a row."

She snapped her head up and looked at him, ready to get irritated over his sarcasm.

But somehow, she couldn't. He was smiling at her now, and his teeth were so white and his eyes were so warm that she just couldn't think about being angry. All she could think about was being...

Attracted.

Maybe Joe was the guy for her, after all.

And maybe he did like her, after all.

He was certainly acting like he did.

Maybe he was just shy about making the first move....

Or maybe after everything that had happened, with the music store and everything, he thought she wasn't interested in him.

Well, it was time for her to take charge of her life in every aspect, wasn't it? Time to get back on track, to figure out what she wanted and go after it.

She wanted Joe, she realized.

Why had she been denying that from the start, trying to convince herself that he wasn't her type? It would do her good to go out with someone nice, and decent, and smart. It would be in keeping with her new lifestyle.

She should let him know, in some subtle way, that she was interested in him.

"Hey, Joe," she heard herself saying, "you want to do something, sometime?"

"Do something?" he echoed.

"Yeah," she said hesitantly, wondering what the hell she was doing.

This wasn't exactly subtle.

But it was too late to back out, so she plunged on, full speed ahead.

"Like, maybe I could come to your soccer game, and afterward, we can go out for a dri—coffee," she amended hastily, figuring Joe wasn't the type who would hang out in a bar. "Or a movie."

"You mean, a date?"

"Like that, yeah," she said feebly, not liking the look on his face.

It wasn't just surprise....

It was...

Dismay?

"Kim," he said after a moment, "I have a girlfriend."

"You do?" She felt her face grow flaming in the space of a second.

"Delia," he said.

"The redhead in history class?"

He frowned. "Oh, Missy? No, she's just a friend. I've been going out with Delia since high school. She goes to school in Massachusetts."

"Oh..." Kim was mortified. How could she have made such a stupid mistake? How could she have thought Joe might be interested in her? Just because he'd talked to her a few times?

He talked to everyone. Missy, and... everyone. He was just a nice guy, that was all.

"I'm really sorry, Kim."

It would have been easier if he looked as flustered as she

felt—or even if he looked mildly flustered. But he didn't. He was calm and casual, as though girls asked him out every day.

They probably did.

But Kim had never gone out on a limb like this before. She'd taken a huge chance...

And fallen flat on her face.

And now here he was, apologizing, as though she were positively crushed that he was already taken.

Well, she wasn't.

"It's no big deal," she heard herself saying. "I'll see you later, okay? I've got to get to algebra."

"Yeah, later," he called after her. "At the soccer game, right?"

Yeah, right, she thought grimly as she hurried away. *I wouldn't go to your soccer game if you paid me....*

And that was really saying something, considering how desperate she was for money.

Kim had been to O'Donnell's Tavern twice in her life, and never in the afternoon. The rundown bar on the edge of town was famous for not asking college students for I.D.

Unlike the few quaint pubs along Main Street, with their brass fixtures, ceiling fans, and frozen drink specials, O'Donnell's was a dive, strictly for serious drinking, not socializing.

Which was fine with Kim.

She wasn't interested in socializing.

Not after what had just happened with Joe.

All she wanted to do, as she stepped into the dimly lit bar, was drown her sorrows.

Alone.

Thankfully, the place was empty, except for the lone bartender who was perched on a stool, watching a soap opera on the portable television above the bar.

This is pathetic, Kim thought, pulling out a stool. The top felt sticky, and she hesitated, then took off her jean jacket and spread it across the peeling Naugahyde.

She lit a cigarette and ordered a draft, and as she watched the silent bartender fill a glass at the tap, she decided she'd sunk to an all-time low.

Never in her life had she come to a bar alone, or even had a drink alone.

In fact...

Wasn't that one of the warning signs of alcoholism?

A sick feeling took hold in the pit of her stomach as the bartender set the beer down in front of her.

"Buck-fifty," he said.

"Can I run a tab?" She had seven dollars and change in her pocket, which could get her nicely buzzed. And Suzy's check should be arriving in today's mail, so it didn't matter if she spent every cent.

He nodded and walked away.

Kim reached for the glass. It was water-spotted and there was a faint smudge of lipstick along the top edge.

Kim eyed it with distaste, wondering if she should ask for another glass.

No. The next one could be worse, she thought.

Well, maybe she just shouldn't drink it.

No. She had to drink it. That was why she was here.

Things were pretty bad, she thought, picking it up. What harm could it do to escape, just for a little while?

She sipped the beer and found it lukewarm and slightly flat. Big surprise.

The bartender had gone back to his soap opera, apparently not the least bit fazed by the presence of a down-and-out eighteen-year-old.

No, you're not exactly down and out, Kim amended. *You're just...*

Down.

And who wouldn't be, after a couple of days like she'd just endured?

She mentally ran down the list of reasons she should be here, drinking alone.

A housemate who had stolen all her bill money, jeopardized her personal credit record, and then nearly gotten her arrested in a drug bust.

Another housemate who had moved out with no notice just before the rent was due.

A teacher who refused to bend her rules even slightly and would probably give Kim's paper a failing grade.

A guy who had flirted outrageously with her and led her on—

Yes, he did, she argued mentally with a nagging little voice that protested that Joe hadn't done anything of the sort—

Only to turn her down when she worked up her nerve to ask him out.

And a father who had never been there for her, and never would be.

Kim took another sip of her beer and another drag on her cigarette and felt sorrier than ever for herself.

Every part of her life was screwed up.

Her finances.

Her living situation.

Her academic situation.

Her family life.

Her love life.

What was left?

Oh, yeah. She might be on her way to becoming an alcoholic.

She set the glass down and stared glumly off into space, wondering how things could possibly be worse.

The door to the bar opened, and someone walked in. She didn't even glance in his direction until she heard a voice say, "Hey, I know you."

She looked up and recognized Kevin's friend Random. "Hi," she said curtly, because she had to say something.

"Never seen you in here before. Shouldn't you be at school or something?"

"Shouldn't you?"

"I don't go to school," he said, and she wondered why she was surprised. She'd assumed that was how Kevin knew him.

But then, what would a guy like Random be doing in college? She couldn't picture him in a classroom, or carrying books around, or taking tests.

No, a guy like Random—an obvious loser—belonged here, in a seedy bar in the middle of the afternoon.

And what does that make you? a nagging voice asked, and Kim cringed.

"So what's up?" he asked after ordering a double shot of Jack Daniel's.

She shrugged, wanting to tell him to get lost, but afraid to. He didn't seem like the kind of guy who would take kindly to that.

He slid onto the stool next to her, and she could smell the pungent scent of weed clinging to his hooded sweatshirt and jeans. She wondered if all he ever did was get high, then realized that for the first time, she could understand how someone could end up that way.

For all she knew, Random's life was even more messed up than her own. He might have had problems, really deep-seated emotional stuff, that had set him on a self-destructive course.

She looked up at him and saw that he was studying her, his bright blue pupils piercing and glassy.

"What?" she said, unnerved by his stare.

"You look in a bad way. Anyone ever told you you look like you could use some help?"

"What kind of help?" A warning bell went off in her mind. She knew what it meant when a guy like Random referred to "help."

He shrugged. "First, tell me what's up."

"Where do you want me to start?"

"It's that bad?"

"You should know. It's partly your fault."

"What do you mean?" He narrowed his eyes at her, then tossed back his shot of Jack and beckoned to the bartender for another one.

"You and your buddy Kevin really screwed up."

"Kevin's not my buddy."

"Really? I thought you were his supplier," she said daringly, putting out her cigarette and spinning her glass of beer in a circle on the bar.

"What gave you that idea?"

"I'm not an idiot."

"Well, neither am I. But Kevin's a different story, man. He owed me big time, and then he flaked out on me."

"Owed you what? Money?"

Random shrugged. "What else is there?"

"Yeah, that's for sure." Kim took another sip of her beer. For some reason, it wasn't going down as easily as she'd anticipated, and it wasn't just that the stuff was warm and flat.

"So what's up with Kevin?" she asked Random. "Is he still in jail?"

"Dude's gonna be in jail for a long time," he gloated.

"What about you?"

"What about me?"

"How do you know you won't get caught, too?"

He looked her in the eye. "Because I haven't done anything wrong."

"Yeah, right." She broke his gaze and glanced again at her beer.

"So what do you need?" he asked.

"What do you mean?"

"You're down. People who are down need to be picked up. You want to be up?"

She looked at him. "I don't think so."

"You don't sound so sure."

She didn't?

"I don't?" she asked, frowning. "Look, Random, I don't do drugs. That's one thing I refuse to get into. I have enough problems."

He downed the second shot the bartender put in front of him, then stood up. "Yeah, well, if you change your mind, you know where to find me."

"I won't change my mind. And anyway, I have no clue where to find you."

"Here. I stop in every afternoon for a little relaxation. And I live right down the street, above the Laundromat."

"Well, I won't change my mind, so it doesn't matter."

He shrugged and started for the door. "Don't forget to check your pockets."

"What?"

"You'll figure it out," he said, and left.

She sighed and reached again for her glass, thinking that he must be pretty out of it, because he wasn't making any sense, talking about pockets.

The beer tasted acrid and she couldn't force down more than one swallow.

She stood up, threw two dollars down on the bar, and left without so much as an acknowledgment from the bartender.

The afternoon had grown chilly, and the sky was gray. It always seemed to be gray these days, Kim thought, pulling her jean jacket on and starting down the street.

Gray, like her mood.

She wondered where she was headed.

Home?

She didn't feel like going back and facing Beryl. Her friend would want to talk, and that was the last thing Kim wanted to do.

She *should* head back to campus, since she had an afternoon English class.

No, *that* was the *last* thing she wanted to do, she decided. Sit there in some classroom and listen to some boring instructor drone on and on about literature or grammar or whatever it was that they were covering these days.

But you promised yourself you were going to start going to classes, nagged that tiny voice. *All of them.*

Well, it was too late for that. She'd already missed algebra so many times she was probably kicked out, since attendance was required.

You blew it, she told herself, and felt tears welling up in her eyes.

That upset her even more. She had never been a crier— never let things get her down to the point where she went around spilling tears in public.

She sniffled and wiped at her eyes and raised her chin stubbornly.

She wasn't going to cry.

She *refused* to cry.

Especially in front of the dirty-faced little kids who were clustered on the porch of a run-down house she was passing.

Poor kids, growing up in such a lousy neighborhood, she thought, then heard them snickering. Were they laughing at her?

Brats, she thought.

She passed a tattoo parlor, then another dive bar.

Things were pretty grim in this part of town. The houses and stores were shabby, some of them even boarded up, and there wasn't a tree or a patch of grass in sight.

She went by a Laundromat, and realized it must be the one Random had mentioned.

This seemed like the perfect dwelling for a drug dealer. Grim. Seedy. Remote.

I have to get away from here, Kim thought, reaching the corner.

But where am I going? she wondered again.

Someplace where I can get my mind off my problems.

Someplace that'll make me feel better.

Where? she wondered again, feeling despair rising in her throat, threatening to choke her.

She stood there on the corner, the chilly wind stirring her hair. She shivered slightly and shoved her hands into the pockets of her jean jacket.

That was when she felt the small, smooth objects deep inside the right pocket, nestled in the corner along the seams.

Kim frowned and pulled them out.

In her hand were two oblong pills.

Chapter 11

Beryl wasn't home when Kim got there Thursday evening.

She wasn't sure whether she was sorry, or glad, to have the place to herself.

She flipped through the mail on the kitchen table and saw that the check from her mother was there. Suzy had scribbled a short note on a yellow Post-it™ that said, *Here's enough for November rent, and a little extra—treat yourself to something fun.*

Kim tossed the note and check aside, took off her jean jacket, and hung it over the back of a kitchen chair. She stood there looking at it for a minute.

Then she went into the bedroom. She was changing into a pair of sweatpants when the phone rang. She looked all over for the cordless receiver, tracing the rings back to the kitchen. The phone was sitting in the charger base on the counter for a change, right where it should be.

"Hello?"

"Kim?"

"Mom?"

"How are you?"

"I'm..." She let out a shaky sigh. "I'm, you know...fine. Why are you calling? I mean, is something—"

"Everything's fine. In fact, everything's *great*. Gary asked me to go out again this weekend. He's taking me to see *Mamma Mia!* up in Toronto. I'm so excited, Kim."

"That's really...nice."

"We're spending the weekend there, in a fancy hotel right on Yonge Street. And we're going to dinner at some restaurant that spins around up in a tower...."

"Sounds nice, Mom."

"Gary's really incredible. Do you know what was waiting for me when I got back on Sunday?"

"No..."

"A vase of roses, with a card that said, 'I've missed you.' He signed it, 'Love, Gary.'"

Kim thought of warning Suzy not to fall head over heels too fast, then realized it was probably too late.

And anyway, Suzy was a big girl....

And Kim was the last person who should be giving advice.

"Well, I shouldn't run up too big a phone bill," her mother

said. "I just wanted to tell you that I had a great time over the weekend, Kim. I'm so proud of you."

"You are?" Kim sat on the edge of a kitchen chair and fingered the cuff of her jean jacket. "Why?"

"Why wouldn't I be? There you are, far from home, living on your own, going to a big university. It's what I always wanted for you," Suzy said, then gave a little laugh. "Hell, it's what I always wanted for *me*."

"I know, Mom. . . ."

"I'm so glad you have the chance to do this, Kim. You should hear me brag about you to everyone in the office."

"You . . . brag about me?"

"Sure. I tell everyone my daughter goes to Summervale University, and that she's going to be a big, big deal someday. A real success."

"Mom," Kim protested weakly.

"Kim, you are. I can just feel it."

"Mom, you should go. Your phone bill's going to be huge. And you didn't have to send me extra money."

"I wanted to. You deserve a treat once in a while."

"But we can't afford it."

"So I'll skip lunch one or two times to pay for it. Not a big deal," Suzy said in a lighthearted, giddy voice she never used when talking about money.

"Thanks for calling, Mom."

"I love you, Kim."

"You, too."

She hung up the phone and stood in the middle of the kitchen floor.

Then she sighed and went back to her room to finish changing.

Beryl came home late that evening, looking exhausted.

"Where have you been?" Kim asked. She was on the couch, idly staring at an episode of *Punk'd* on MTV.

"At the library, studying. I have a major test in the morning."

"So do I."

"In what?"

"History."

"Did you study?"

"How can I study? I don't have the textbook."

"Don't you know anyone in the class you can study with?"

She thought fleetingly of Joe. "No."

"Well, isn't the text on reserve in the library?"

"What do you mean?"

"Didn't your professor tell you on the first day of class that the book was in the library? They usually do that."

"Well, why didn't you tell me before now?"

Beryl looked irked. "Because it's not up to me to tell you, Kim. I'm not responsible for making sure you get your work done. And anyway, the professor probably told you. You probably didn't hear her."

"She didn't say anything about a text being reserved in the

library," Kim said, though she wasn't nearly as certain as she sounded.

"Look, Kim," Beryl said, sitting heavily. "You can't go around not turning in papers and failing tests. It's going to catch up with you at some point."

"Yeah, I know."

"Well, then, do something about it."

"Beryl, I'm trying. But no matter what I do, I fall flat on my face again. I just can't seem to get it together. I'm trying, but it's like fate is against me."

"You are not trying, Kim," Beryl told her.

Kim stared at her. "*What?*"

"You're not trying. You *say* you are, but you're not. Not really. You act like things are beyond your control, but they're not."

"What's that supposed to mean?"

"Think about it."

"I am thinking about it. I don't get it."

"Then think about it for a while." Beryl stood and picked up her bookbag. "I have to go change. I'm going out."

"Where?"

"There's a party at the Kappa House."

"I didn't know that. Maybe I'll come." Kim picked up the remote control, turned off the television, and stood up.

"Are you sure you want to do that?"

Kim stared at Beryl. "What are you talking about?"

"If you don't know, then it wouldn't help if I explained

it," Beryl said, shaking her head and starting to leave the room.

"God, what's with you?" Kim called after her.

"I just can't deal with watching you sit around feeling sorry for yourself anymore," Beryl said. Then she turned and looked over her shoulder, her expression softening. "And anyway, I have PMS. And I gained five pounds. I'm in a shitty mood."

"Well, don't take it out on me," Kim said, sitting on the couch again.

"Sorry." Beryl disappeared into their bedroom.

Kim turned the television on again.

The people on *Punk'd* were so perky and energized she couldn't stand watching them anymore. She flipped from station to station, vetoing every program, then turned off the television.

Beryl emerged from the bedroom, dressed in jeans and a tight black turtleneck. "Do I look fat?" she asked Kim.

"No."

"Are you sure?"

"Yes."

"Yeah, right. I'm totally bloated. So are you coming?"

Kim looked up again at her. "I thought you didn't want me to."

"It's not that. I just—never mind. Are you coming?"

"No. I don't feel like a party tonight," Kim said truthfully.

Beryl shrugged. "I'll see you later."

"See you."

Alone in the silent apartment, Kim sighed.

She got up and wandered again to the kitchen, where her jacket was still slung over the chair.

She picked it up, toyed with it for a minute, and put it down again.

It slid off the back of the chair, into a heap on the floor.

Kim retrieved it, and saw that the two pills had fallen out of the pocket. They sat there on the linoleum, as if daring her to pick them up.

And take them.

What would happen if she did?

Would she become a drug-crazed addict?

The idea was so ludicrous she had to smile.

You'll probably just feel warm and happy, she told herself.

Warm and happy.

When was the last time she had felt that way?

She couldn't even remember.

She bent and picked up the pills, holding them in her open hand.

How dangerous could two tiny things be? she wondered. It wasn't as if she'd get hooked, and anyway, she didn't have any more. It would just be this one time.

Maybe they would help.

After all, didn't doctors prescribe medication for people who were depressed? This was no different, except that she'd gotten the pills without a prescription.

She looked over at the sink. All she had to do was fill a glass with water, pop the pills into her mouth, and gulp them down.

It would be that easy.

She closed her hand and jiggled the pills, hearing the slight tapping noise they made in her fist.

She wanted to escape, didn't she?

Tonight, this was the only escape she had.

You act like things are beyond your control, but they're not.

For some reason, Beryl's words popped into her head.

She tried to shove them out, but there they were, echoing over and over.

For a long time, Kim stood there in the kitchen, staring at the pills in her hand.

Then she went to the sink and turned on the water.

You act like things are beyond your control, but they're not.

She opened her fist and looked at the pills.

Then she turned her hand, letting them fall out into the sink, where the rush of water swept them swiftly down the drain.

West Twelfth Street was ominously deserted in the wee hours of the morning.

As Kim made her way along the block, she pulled her jean jacket closer around her neck, trying to shut out the chill wind.

In only a few more days, it would be November.

She would be going home for Thanksgiving in a few weeks. Her mother would want to know all about school, how she was doing in her classes and whether she had decided on a major yet.

She wouldn't be able to use a mounting long-distance telephone tab as an excuse to cut the conversation short.

Her friends would be there, too, eager to tell her about
their lives at college, and wanting to hear about hers.

Kim had looked forward to their reunion ever since they'd
said goodbye in September.

She wanted to keep looking forward to it.

She wanted to keep looking *forward*.

That was the key.

She turned the corner and continued walking through the
predawn shadows, walking with a sense of purpose for the
first time in...

Well, in a long time.

Too long.

Ten minutes later she reached her destination.

The Hop was lit in neon pink against the sky, and a matching smear of pinkish glow had appeared on the horizon.

Dawn was breaking, Kim realized, looking up at it.

She smiled.

She opened the door and stepped from the quiet street
into the restaurant's crowded, welcoming din.

She spotted the waitress she'd met yesterday morning—
God, had it only been twenty-four hours ago?

Kim made her way over to the counter and touched
the woman on the sleeve of her white uniform as she
passed by.

"I'll be with you in a moment, hon," she said hurriedly.
"Why don't you have a seat."

"No," Kim said, "I'm here to see Fritz...about the job."

The woman grinned. "I'll get him."

The lecture hall was filled with students.

Kim made her way down the aisle, looking for a vacant seat toward the front.

There had been a few in back, but she'd told herself she wasn't going to do that.

Not anymore.

She spotted an empty desk and headed for it, then realized Joe was seated beside it. A familiar redhead was on his other side, and she appeared to be chattering to him.

Kim hesitated in the aisle, then boldly raised her chin and slid into the row. She made her way to the seat and sat just as Joe turned. A look of surprise—pleasant surprise—came over his features.

"Hey," he said, "you missed my game yesterday."

"Sorry...I was busy." Could he tell her voice was trembling?

He grinned. "We lost, so you didn't miss much, although I managed to score a goal."

"Good for you."

"Hey, Kim, this is Missy," he said, gesturing at the girl beside him. "Missy, Kim."

"Hi," Kim said, and the girl smiled cheerfully.

"Did you study?" she asked Kim.

"Yup. I've been in the library all morning."

"It's only ten o'clock," Missy pointed out.

"I get up early."

"Really?" Joe looked surprised. "I thought you liked to sleep in."

"I did, but...I guess I won't be doing that for a while."

"Why not?"

"I got that job at the Hop."

"You did?" He looked surprised. "I thought you weren't looking for work."

"I lied," she said with a shrug.

She wanted to add, *But I've decided not to do that anymore. I've decided not to do a lot of things anymore.*

But Dr. Armstrong had walked into the classroom and taken her place at the front. She was carrying a sheaf of papers in one arm, and a familiar-looking document in her other hand.

She looked up, scanning the back of the lecture hall, and Kim saw an expression of disappointment come into the instructor's eyes.

She rose slightly from her seat and raised her arm.

Dr. Armstrong's gaze fell on her, and she smiled.

"Kim," she called, and beckoned her to the front of the room.

"What's going on?" Joe asked, beside her, as she got up.

"I think Dr. Armstrong has something for me."

He nodded and went back to talking to Missy as Kim made her way down the row and down the aisle to the waiting instructor.

"Here's your essay," Dr. Armstrong said, handing her the paper-clipped stack of notebook paper.

"Thank you." Kim took it, afraid to glance down at it.

She turned to go back to her seat.

"Kim?" Dr. Armstrong said.

"Yes?" She spun around again.

"I'm sorry I had to mark it down for lateness and for not typing. It would have been an A."

It took a moment for the words to sink in.

Then Kim's heart soared. She looked down at the paper and saw that Dr. Armstrong had given her a B-plus.

"Thank you," she said, breaking into a grin.

"Next time, you'll get an A. Correct?" Dr. Armstrong asked.

"Definitely."

"Are you ready for the test?"

Kim nodded, still smiling.

"Good. Please take your seat. We're ready to begin."

As she made her way back up the aisle, Kim's footsteps were light and her heart was sailing.

"You look happy," Joe observed in a whisper as she slid into her seat again.

"I am happy," she told him. "Very happy."

"You must have gotten a good grade on your paper."

"I did," Kim said.

But it was more than that.

So much more.

She was in charge of her life once again. She wasn't foolish enough to think the next few weeks would be easy. She had several professors to meet with, and a lot of makeup work to do—*if* they agreed to keep her enrolled in their courses.

But she was going to do everything in her power to convince them that she deserved another chance.

And she was going to make the most of the chances she got.

That, she promised herself, was the way things should be...

And the way they were going to stay from now on.

Now a Berkley Jam paperback

Maybe joining a sorority wasn't the best idea, after all...

College Life 101
CAMERON: The Sorority

National Bestselling Author
Wendy Corsi Staub
0-425-19727-1

And don't miss:
College Life 101
ZARA: The Roommate
0-425-19914-2

It's the hottest summer job ever...

HOT TRASH

Cherie Bennett & Jeff Gottesfeld

Six girls and boys are about to have one hot summer. They've been chosen to move to New York City to be interns on the new reality talk show *Trash*.

But what goes on while the cameras are rolling is nothing compared to the happenings behind the lights.

Includes the first two books in the popular series:
Trash and
Love, Lies, and Video

0-425-20120-1
www.penguin.com

LOOK FOR THESE TOTALLY
FRESH BOOKS FROM

berkley jam

COMING JULY 2005
*CONFESSIONS OF AN
ALMOST-MOVIE STAR*
BY MARY KENNEDY
0-425-20467-7

COMING AUGUST 2005
*JENNIFER SCALES AND
THE ANCIENT FURNACE*
BY MARYJANICE DAVIDSON
AND ANTHONY ALONGI
0-425-20598-3